Three-in-One
Hazel Townson
Stories

Ⓐ

Andersen Press • London

Published in 2004 by Andersen Press Limited,
20 Vauxhall Bridge Road, London SW1V 2SA

Break-In was first published in 1997 by
Andersen Press Limited
Text copyright © 1997 by Hazel Townson
Illustrations copyright © 1997 by David McKee

Danny - Don't Jump! was first published in 1985 by
Andersen Press Limited
Text copyright © 1985 by Hazel Townson
Illustrations copyright © 1985 by Amelia Rosato

One Green Bottle was first published in 1987 by
Andersen Press Limited
Text copyright © 1987 by Hazel Townson
Illustrations copyright © 1987 by David McKee

Cover illustration copyright © 2004 by Tony Ross

The moral rights of author and illustrators have been asserted

British Library Cataloguing in Publication Data available
ISBN 1 84270 440 0

Printed and bound in Great Britain by
Bookmarque Ltd, Croydon, Surrey

Contents

Hazel Townson

BREAK-IN

Illustrated by David McKee

Andersen Press · London

Contents

For Greta Short

1
Deaf Ears

'Why don't you LISTEN?' Mrs Butler yelled at her son Jack. 'You never listen! Or if you do, it goes in at one ear and out at the other. I told you not to wear that tee-shirt any more; it's falling to bits. Where's that nice new Superman one I bought you last week?' Turning to Jack's dad, she added: 'I don't know why I bother talking to that boy. He never listens!'

'You what?' mumbled Dad, absorbed in his newspaper. He hadn't a clue what his wife had just said, but guessed she was rattling on at poor old Jack again. He peeped round the corner of the page and gave his son a consoling wink.

'I'm going round to Sam's,' Jack announced sulkily.

'Not in that tee-shirt, you're not! What-ever would Samantha's mother think? And I wish you'd stop calling her Sam; it makes her sound like a tomboy.'

'No, it doesn't! She likes being called Sam; it was her idea,' Jack protested hotly. 'And I'm not wearing stupid Superman. It's baby stuff. Other kids have mums who let them pick their own clothes instead of forcing them to wear stuff they hate.'

Mrs Butler glared at her son in outraged astonishment.

'What did you say?'

Jack suddenly lost his temper. 'If you don't know, you should listen! You never listen!' he shouted, rushing away. From the safety of the doorway he added with reckless cheek: 'It goes in at one ear and out at the other.'

Jack Butler didn't usually behave so badly. What on earth had come over him? He must have gone mad, asking for trouble like that!

Besides, when he'd calmed down a bit he had to admit that his mother was right; he didn't always hear what was said, partly because he was usually playing his mouth-organ. He hadn't been playing it today though, and he certainly hadn't heard a word about tee-shirts.

Now that he came to think of it, his mother was always using phrases like: 'What did I just tell you?' and 'You never listen!' Did he really miss so much of what was said? Perhaps there was something wrong with his ears? Now, that would be worrying! Suppose he finished up not being able to hear his own mouth-organ? Or Sam's infectious giggle? Or 'Top of the Pops'? Or the ice-cream van coming down the road?

Well, he could still hear the sea, at any rate. Scrambling over the dunes, he reached the long, pale stretch of deserted beach, ran to the water's edge and hurled a pebble at an incoming wave.

Splash! He heard that as well. Plus a couple of seagulls screaming overhead, and a dog barking in the distance.

Was it the fault of his mouth-organ? His mum always claimed his playing was damaging her ear-drums so maybe it was doing the same to his. He took the instrument from his pocket and played an experimental tune which mingled uneasily with the hiss and crash of water and set a gannet fleeing in sheer terror. But no, that wasn't it; his ears felt the same as usual.

Well then, perhaps it was his brain that

was at fault? Could he be the victim of mental black-outs? Temporary loss of memory? Perhaps he had a brain tumour or some other fatal disease that the school nurse, preoccupied with nits, had managed to overlook.

Jack wandered back towards the rocks, chose a flat one for a seat and settled down to think. For the first time in his life he was desperately worried. Did he have a real medical problem here, or was it more a question of stress? He had just decided to go and confide in Sam (who was not only his best friend but also the brainiest girl in school) when suddenly a voice caught his attention.

'Look here, are you prepared to listen, or aren't you?' it demanded in crisp irritation.

Were Jack's ears playing more tricks? There was nobody about. He scanned the empty beach, but the voice came again.

'This is a great idea if you'll just stop moping long enough to listen!'

The sound was coming from the rocks behind him. Jack did stop moping. He stood up and looked around, but there was not a soul in sight. He climbed to a higher point and surveyed the beach once more. Absolutely nobody, which was not unusual first thing on a Monday morning.

Now he sat down again, trembly with panic. His affliction was more serious than he'd thought; he was hallucinating! Unless, of course, the voice belonged to some invisible Guardian Angel who was trying to sort him out. Jack remembered the scary pictures of gigantic angels looming from Sunday School walls, and couldn't decide which idea was the more disturbing. He strained his ears mightily all the same.

'Look, I'm fast losing patience!' the mystery voice continued. 'Here am I with a really brilliant solution to your problem and you keep ignoring me. The least you can do is listen!'

So for once Jack Butler concentrated hard and listened. What he heard gave him the biggest shock of his life.

2
Unwilling Ears

Samantha Platt was also having trouble at home. Her mum's new partner, known to her and Jack as 'Bullying Billy', was laying down the law again.

'I think you should forget about this new girl-friend of yours,' he was saying. 'She lives much too far away.'

The girl-friend in question was Amanda Ross, whom Sam had met during her school's day trip to a stately home. Amanda's school group had also been there, and had joined with Sam's in the conducted tour. Sam and Amanda had started chatting and had really taken to one another. They had shared their picnic lunch and stayed together for the rest of the visit. It had seemed perfectly natural after that to make plans to meet again in the holidays and get to know one another better.

'Come over to my house for the day,' Amanda had invited.

Although Amanda lived nearly twenty miles away, Sam was sure her mum would drive her there.

Amanda wrote her telephone number on the back of Sam's hand and explained that her home would seem a big change from the seaside. The house was deep in the country-side, miles from anywhere.

'Your mum will find it, though; she's sure to have a map. Let me know what time you're coming and I'll be looking out for you.'

Mrs Platt had been quite happy with this arrangement and the journey had been planned for tomorrow. But now Bullying Billy had found out and was determined to stop it.

'Do you realise how far it is to that girl's house? Your mum hasn't time to go gallivanting about all over the countryside just so you can have a day out. Anyway, I'd like to know what makes this girl so much better than the kids in our village. You've been happy enough with them up to now. I thought Jack Butler was your friend?'

'Am I only allowed one friend, then?' Sam snapped angrily.

At this point Mrs Platt, fearing a major row, intervened timidly: 'I don't mind driving her, Billy. Honestly, it's no trouble!'

'Well, I mind. It's not safe for young girls these days to go off to strange places and stop with people we don't know. These folks live miles from civilisation by all accounts; anything could happen. Besides, I might want the car.'

'Ah, now we're getting at the truth!' sneered Sam.

With a warning frown at her daughter, Mrs Platt tried her best to ease the situation.

'It's not that far, Billy. I could drive there and back in an hour.'

'Huh! You'd be lucky! You know what the traffic's like these days, and once you get

past Benswick those country roads will be one-lane-only. You'd be backing up to passing-places all the time. And don't forget you'd have to fetch her home again afterwards, driving right through the middle of Benswick in the rush-hour. You know what that means – snarl-ups, road rage and business-lunch drunks. The whole thing's out of the question.'

'I needn't come home until well after the rush-hour,' suggested Sam.

'That's a selfish idea if ever I heard one! Outstaying your welcome and spoiling your mum's evening into the bargain. That's the only time she gets to have a bit of a rest.'

To cook your dinner and wash it up, you mean, Sam thought mutinously. If anyone was being selfish, she told Billy, it was him, ruining her whole life just because he might have to walk somewhere for once.

'Now, don't exaggerate, Sam,' her mother warned. 'You always have to make a drama out of everything. One little trip isn't that important.'

'Oh, yes it is! We were going to be friends

for life, me and Amanda. Now I'll lose touch with her and I'll never see her again as long as I live.'

'Don't be ridiculous! I never heard such a fuss about a girl you hardly know. You've only met her once,' Billy pointed out.

'Once was enough.'

'You're right there, because you're NOT GOING all that way to see her and that's final. It's time you learned to listen to good advice.'

Bullying Billy had had enough of this argument and as far as he was concerned the matter was closed.

Mrs Platt made one more half-hearted attempt to intervene, but in the end, as usual, she gave in to Billy's bullying and told Sam it was probably for the best.

'You must admit it is a bit far to travel, love, especially when you've got good friends here. I think we should listen to Billy after all.'

'Oh, yes! Let's listen to Billy!' Sam cried angrily. 'That's all we ever do!'

'Billy's only thinking . . .'

'Oh, I know what Billy's thinking,' Sam interrupted bitterly. 'He's thinking, "Let's stop that girl from having any fun. Let's show her who's boss in this house!"'

'Samantha!' cried Mrs Platt in shock. 'How can you say such a wicked thing?'

'Because it's true, that's how! But let me tell you, Amanda's worth ten of you lot any day! I might have to listen to you now, but I won't always have to. And one day you'll wish you hadn't been so rotten.'

'How DARE you?' roared Billy. 'How dare you talk to your mother and me like that? You've got very cheeky lately, young lady, and it's time you were taught a lesson. You just wait till I get home tonight . . .!'

Sam panicked. She'd said more than she intended, and had made a real enemy of Billy now. He was as angry as she'd ever seen him. Before the situation could get any worse, Sam fled.

3
Haunted Rocks

Jack eventually worked out that the voices he was hearing came from a long, jagged gap between the rocks. Among those rocks, hidden somewhere behind or beneath him, were invisible presences whose mutterings were now rising scarily upwards like a genie from a bottle. Could they be the ghosts of dead seamen washed up on the shore, whose bones, picked clean by seabirds, had long since sunk deep into the sand? But no; to his great relief and by dint of careful eaves-dropping Jack at last identified these presences as two ordinary humans. One of them actually sneezed.

Their names turned out to be Baz and

Vic. They were having a serious discussion in some hideaway among the rocks where they were sheltering from the wind and couldn't be seen from the shore. Presumably they thought they would not be overheard either. Vic was the one being told to listen carefully, and Jack, now concentrating hard, soon found out why. Baz was giving Vic instructions for some job they had to do, which gradually revealed itself as the theft of a computer from a school. Jack couldn't hear everything, but the words 'school' and 'computer' and 'break-in' kept on cropping up, and at one point Baz raised his voice and explained quite clearly:

'It's perfect timing, while the school's closed for the summer.'

Well, there was only one school round here, and that was Shoreside Primary, the village school which Jack and Sam attended. Jack's curiosity turned to consternation, then to outrage, as he realised he was actually listening in to a plan to rob his own school!

Shoreside Primary School, small and under-funded, had only thirty-nine pupils and one computer. The computer was almost new; so new, in fact, that the thrill of possession had not yet worn off and the children fought for the chance to use it.

It was not easy for a small village school to acquire such expensive equipment. This machine had been bought from hard-earned money raised through various sponsored efforts by the children. Jack himself had endured agonies of blisters on a sponsored walk, more agonies of hunger through a sponsored fast and even worse agonies of boredom during a sponsored silence. He'd earned so much on this last one that he'd nearly forgotten how to play his mouth-organ! Was all that suffering to turn into a massive wasted effort? Not if he could help it!

Cautiously, he drew closer to the gap in the rocks, but decided he wouldn't be able to peer over at the burglars' hiding place without being seen.

Jack had more sense than to go plunging recklessly into danger, especially with two villains like these on the prowl. But he was determined to save the school's precious computer. The thing to do was to run to the village police station with a warning.

Seathorpe police station was an ordinary cottage in which the local constable lived with his wife and two young children. Jack passed it every day on his way to school. Today, as usual, this split-personality house had nappies and baby clothes blowing on a line in the back garden and a huge DON'T

27

DRINK AND DRIVE! poster in the front window.

The constable's wife was busy sweeping the front path with a smart new red-handled broom.

''Morning, Mrs Lewis,' gasped Jack, out of breath from running. 'Is Constable Lewis in? I've got something to tell him.'

'Well, he's busy just now, Jack. He's writing a report about a missing dog and needs to get it finished. It's important.'

'So's this. I've just found out about a very nasty crime that's going to happen.'

'What, here in Seathorpe?' Mrs Lewis looked amused. Unless the missing dog had been deliberately fed to the sharks, the last nasty crime in this sleepy corner of the globe had been a couple of rude words chalked on the chapel wall.

'It's to do with the school,' insisted Jack. 'It's going to get robbed.'

'Oh, well I suppose you'd better come in.'

Mrs Lewis propped her broom against the garden gate and led Jack into the front room which served as an office. There sat the constable, scribbling away at his desk with a cup of coffee and a half-eaten bun at his elbow.

The constable looked up in surprise.

'Now then, Jack, what can I do for you? Come to make a confession, have you?'

'Jack's got some information about a very nasty crime,' announced Mrs Lewis, trying her best not to smile.

The constable swivelled round in his office chair.

'Now, that should liven the day up!' he grinned. 'Well, go on, boy! Don't keep us in suspense.'

Jack told his story as clearly as he could, leaving nothing out. Yet it was obvious from the start that the constable was not taking him seriously.

'Disembodied voices floating out from a crack in the rocks? Come on now, Jack, are you sure you didn't fall asleep on the beach and dream it all?'

Jack was indignant. He never fell asleep on the beach; there were too many interesting things to do. Anyway, how could he have dreamed it when he even knew the two men's names?

'People don't dream names,' he insisted.

'People can dream anything, boy, including the winning lottery numbers for next week, but it doesn't make it true.'

'Well, I didn't dream it. I heard them, honestly! I heard nearly every word they said.'

'Only "nearly"? Well then, if there *was* somebody there you must have had to strain your ears pretty hard. And you know, my old mum always reckons it's very bad manners to go around listening in to other people's conversations. She says folks who do that only get hold of the wrong end of the stick and cause a lot of trouble all round.'

'My mum's always telling me to *listen*,' Jack complained, fervently wishing the grown-ups would make up their minds what they wanted. 'Anyway, aren't you going to do anything about it?'

'Let's put it this way, Jack. I'm glad you're on the side of the law, and you did right to come and tell me if you thought there was something wrong. I'll keep my eyes open, but I don't think we need to start tearing

the rocks apart or putting SAS cordons round the school, do you? In fact, I don't think you need to worry at all. You probably don't realise it, laddie, but you're living in an almost crime-free zone.'

It was a good thing he said 'almost', for somebody had just stolen the attractive new broom his wife had left propped against the gate.

4
The Missing Dog

So much for this business of listening! thought Jack disgustedly. The Lewises hadn't listened to him properly because right from the start they'd made up their minds not to believe him. Jack could imagine them having a good laugh at his expense the minute he was out of earshot. Well, he'd show them! He'd save the school's computer and maybe catch the burglars into the bargain. He wouldn't need to do it alone either; Sam would help him.

He started off towards Sam's house, but met her running away from it, looking almost as fed-up as he felt. Jack's heart sank. Was Sam in the mood to listen?

Sam not only listened to Jack but she believed every word he said. What's more, she was glad to share somebody else's problem to take her mind off her own.

'Cops are a waste of time,' she declared. 'The person we need to tell is Mr Cronin.'

Mr Cronin was the school caretaker, so school was where they looked for him first.

He was usually busy spring-cleaning the classrooms in the holidays. Finding the building locked and deserted they hurried over to his house, but that too ended in disappointment, for Mr Cronin wasn't at home. His wife said he'd already left for Glasgow, where he was attending his uncle's funeral tomorrow.

'It's too far to go and come back in a day so he's stopping the night with his relatives. I'd have gone with him, except for our Cameron. I expect you've heard that poor old Cammy went missing yesterday?'

Cameron was the Cronins' dog, who looked in at school sometimes and was a great favourite with the children. Mrs Cronin was obviously very upset about his disappearance.

'So I'm stopping at home in case he turns up,' she explained. 'Poor pet, I'm sure something terrible's happened to him. There are some funny people about these days. They'd steal the chimney-pot off your roof if they thought they could sell it, and our Cammy's a thoroughbred. He'd fetch a very good price. I don't suppose you've seen any sign of him on your travels?'

Sam and Jack had to admit they hadn't seen the dog for a couple of days.

'We'll keep an eye out for him, though,' Sam promised as they walked away.

Jack was impressed by that remark about funny people, for his mind was still on Baz and Vic. He thought Mr Cronin would have believed him. What's more, as a responsible caretaker Mr Cronin would have kept a special lookout at school if he'd been here tonight. Come to think of it, that was probably why those two had turned up today. They must have found out about the funeral and known the coast would be clear.

Just as Jack was feeling desperate, Sam suddenly declared: 'It's up to us, then!' After a minute's thought, she added: 'Let's ask Mrs Cronin if we can borrow the school keys. Then we could set a booby-trap. Or we could hide the computer where they'd never find it.'

'You must be joking; she'll never let us in school on our own.'

Jack was right; Mrs Cronin was aghast at the very idea. 'Oooh, no, I can't let you have the keys! It's more than my husband's job's worth to let those keys out of his sight. And when he's not here, they're in my charge. It's a very big responsibility!'

'You could come in to school with us,' suggested Sam, 'then you can see we're not getting up to any mischief.' She explained what they were intending to do.

'Gracious me, I call that mischief!' Mrs Cronin was even more horrified. Nobody was to touch that computer unless a teacher was present; those were her husband's instructions. He wasn't even allowed to lift it up to dust underneath it, which was a very slovenly state of affairs. As for booby traps, they were downright dangerous, and those who laid such things might well get caught in them, and serve them right! Anyway, the person to deal with robbers was Constable Lewis.

'I've tried him but he doesn't believe me,' Jack told her. 'And we can't just let the school get robbed.'

'Don't you worry, the school won't get robbed. It's all locked up and alarmed. Even James Bond couldn't get in there, believe me!'

'Do you think that's true?' Jack asked Sam as they trailed away disappointed.

'We'll just have to hope so, though Bullying Billy reckons nothing stops a determined villain – and he should know! Anyway, right now I can't think what else we can do. We can't hang about outside school in the middle of the night when we're supposed to be in bed. Even if we did, we'd be asking for trouble. Goodness knows what people like that would do if they caught us.'

'You mean we've just got to let them get away with it?' Jack reminded Sam of all the trouble they had taken to get that computer in the first place.

'Well, don't give up hope yet. For a start, the computer might be insured, then the school can replace it. Or we might have a brainwave.'

'Yeah, that's what we need – a brainwave!' Jack decided that if they stopped

thinking about it, an idea might pop up when they least expected it.

Sam had had a similar thought. 'Let's walk over to Pearson's for an ice cream,' she suggested. 'Food's good for ideas, especially sweet stuff. We can keep an eye out for Cameron on the way.'

Jack had suddenly remembered that Constable Lewis was involved with a lost dog, which must be Cameron. It would serve the constable right if they found the dog before he did. Maybe he'd start taking them seriously then.

5
More Voices

Pearson's Point was the name given to a high cliff at the end of the village, from which there was a stunning view of the coastline from Cowslip Bay right round to Seathorpe. Coach-parties often stopped there to take photographs and to sample the refreshments at Pearson's Parlour, the snack-bar perched on top of the cliff.

The day was warm and sunny and the little Parlour was already quite busy. The children ordered a couple of Pearson Specials served in tall glasses with cream, cherries and sunshades on top of multi-coloured ices, and were happily digging in their long spoons when Jack suddenly pricked up his ears. He had heard a voice he recognised.

'So I've got you to listen at last!' declared the voice triumphantly.

Slowly Jack turned round and cast a glance at the couple sitting at the next table. But no; it couldn't be Baz and Vic, for one of these two was a woman.

Jack might have lost interest at this point, except that the man suddenly told the woman: 'Honestly, Vic, you've got no confidence in yourself. What's the problem? I can't see any snags. You've nothing to lose and all to gain.'

Oh, that was Baz's voice all right! Evidently he was still trying to persuade his partner in crime. And why shouldn't that partner be a woman? Vic could be short for Victoria. Jack had to admit that he'd only heard Vic's voice once, whispering the one word 'Baz . . .!' He'd just assumed Vic was a man's name, but after all, Samantha called herself Sam.

'Hey, it's them!' Jack nudged his friend and swivelled his eyes significantly towards the next table.

'I thought you said two men?'

'I said Baz and Vic!' Jack corrected somewhat unfairly, whereupon Baz and Vic got up and began to walk away.

'Come on, then!' cried Sam, leaping to follow them without so much as a backward glance at her half-eaten Pearson Special. Bullying Billy might have done her out of one adventure, but here was another which he couldn't spoil.

Baz and Vic had left a white van in the car park and were already climbing into it as the children rushed outside.

Not having a pen, Sam bent down for a couple of bits of stone, one small and sharp to write with, the other a flat surface. Scratching a note of the van's registration number, she slipped the two stones into her pocket as the van moved off.

'They're heading for Seathorpe.'

'To pinch our computer,' agreed Jack miserably, 'and there's no way we can catch 'em up now.'

'I've got their number, though.'

'So what? Constable Lewis won't do any-

thing if you give it to him.'

'Maybe not now, but when those two have done their thieving he'll be able to track 'em down, and it'll all be our doing. He'll certainly owe us one.'

Jack pondered this new possibility.

'Could be! And if we find Cameron as well . . .!' The day was definitely looking brighter.

As they started back along the road, Sam began telling Jack about her own disappointment and the fight with Bullying Billy.

'Why do we always have to listen to the grown-ups?' she demanded sulkily.

'You tell me!' replied Jack with feeling.

To cheer them up he took out his mouthorgan and began to play a series of what he thought were Irish reels, but the only thing that reeled was a terrified seagull. Fortunately for Sam, at long last Jack stopped in mid-note. For when they least expected it they rounded a bend in the road and came upon a white van parked in a grassy lay-by.

'It's them all right!' Sam checked her stone to make sure the numbers were the same.

'Why do you think they've stopped here?'

'Waiting till dark, I expect. Just keep walking. Pretend we've not noticed them, then they might not notice us.'

'It's all right; they didn't spot me on the beach. They don't know who we are.'

'Well, we know who they are, and with people like that you can't be too careful.'

But the children needn't have worried; Baz and Vic had already left the van. With their backs to the road they were struggling away across a muddy field that led up to Smart's farm. The van stood abandoned with its cab doors locked. Yet the children soon discovered that the rear doors had been left a few centimetres ajar, their handles looped loosely together with string.

'Wonder what they've already pinched?' whispered Jack. 'Let's have a quick look.'

Cautiously the children approached the van.

'Hey – can you hear something?' Jack suddenly stood still and listened. Were his ears playing tricks again, or was there a whimpering noise coming from the back of the van?

'Yeah – there's a dog in there. Probably a Rottweiler so you just watch it!' Sam warned as Jack reached out for the doors.

'That's no Rottweiler. It sounds like a little dog, and he'll be half suffocated, a hot day like this.'

'No, he won't; that's why they've left the doors ajar. If they've got stolen stuff in there he's probably their guard dog.'

'Never! He'd have heard us and gone mad by now,' said Jack. 'Hey, what if it's Cameron?'

Jack moved right up to the van and put his eye to the opening between the doors.

'It *is* Cameron! He's been dognapped! Come on, we've got to get him out!'

'Well, be quick before they come back!'

Feverishly Jack struggled to undo the string and open the doors properly while Sam kept a lookout round the side of the van.

'Hurry up! They've called at Smart's farm but I think they're coming back now. Yeah,

they're crossing the field.'

'I'm being as quick as I can.'

Jack finally pulled the doors apart.
Cameron, who was lying on top of a huge,
untidy heap of tarpaulin, whimpered for-

lornly and made some attempt to struggle free as Jack climbed into the van.

'Hey, Sam! He's injured!'

Sam ran to look and saw that the dog had a makeshift bloodstained bandage on his paw and more blood on his fur. She was so outraged that she forgot to keep watch and climbed into the van to take a closer look.

'Some people are really cruel! How could they do such a thing?'

Sam crouched down beside the dog and talked to him, stroking him gently. Cameron's tail gave a feeble twitch.

'It's all right, boy, we'll soon have you out of here!' promised Sam.

The dog was tied up with string to a metal ring set in the side of the van.

'I can't undo it! Give me that sharp stone you picked up!' ordered Jack.

He sawed fiercely at the string until it frayed, and had just lifted Cameron out on to the grass when there came the sound of voices growing steadily louder. Baz and Vic

had almost reached the van. The children
were caught.

6
A Terrifying Ride

'Hey! Somebody's opened the doors!' cried Vic, running round towards the back of the van.

Now the children were really scared. They had hoped to leap out after Cameron, but Baz and Vic had reappeared too quickly. Any attempt to run away now was sure to end in disaster.

There was only one thing to do. With a quick, silent signal to Sam, Jack lifted one edge of the tarpaulin and began to crawl under it. Sam followed suit, and they both crouched very still in its rubbery folds, holding their breath and trying not to mind the smell.

As for Cameron, he had no intention of hanging around that van a moment longer. Injured or not, he was so glad to be set free that he dragged himself painfully off into the safety of the long grass.

Vic peered into the van.

'Baz! The dog's missing! There's blood on the step. How the dickens did he get out?'

Baz didn't seem to care. 'Probably chewed through the string, or tugged it loose.

Must've been stronger than we thought.'

'But he can't have opened the doors on his own.'

'Maybe the string snapped. But look, we can't spend any more time on that animal, we're already running late. It'll have to take its chances.'

'If you say so!' Vic shrugged, locked the rear doors and climbed into the passenger seat. The children had had no chance to make a move before the van drove off.

There began a rough journey over bumpy country roads, during which the children suffered both discomfort and alarm. Where were they heading? And what would happen when the van eventually stopped? They had realised too late that hiding under the tarpaulin had been a very stupid and dangerous move.

Jack was just imagining his own spectacular funeral (for which his sobbing mother had dressed him in the Superman tee-shirt with matching tights, cape and boots) when the van pulled up with a final swerve outside a solitary country cottage.

Baz ordered Vic to go round and unlock the back doors of the van, leaving them open ready to load up. (Load up with what? the children wondered.) Then both adults walked up to the cottage door.

After a brief pause first Sam's head, then Jack's, emerged from beneath the tarpaulin.

'Quick! Now's our chance!'

Jack let go a giant sneeze he had been holding on to desperately for the last few minutes. Then another sneeze, and another.

'Hold your nose!' Sam whispered anxiously.

'It's all this dust!'

Jack gave another sneeze as Sam grabbed his arm and dragged him towards the rear of the van. She could hardly believe their luck that its doors were now wide open.

Wild with relief, they scrambled out on to the road and dived in among a thick cluster of trees which bordered the roadside opposite the house.

'Where are we?'

Jack stared around but he hadn't a clue. All he could see beyond the trees was wooded countryside with not another house in sight. There was nowhere to run for help. It seemed as if they would just have to follow the road back the way they had come.

Jack wanted to make a start at once, but Sam thought they ought to keep an eye on the villains first, to find out what they were really up to.

'We'll have to be proper witnesses if we want anybody to believe us, and you never know, there might even be a reward.'

By now Baz had rung the doorbell several times without getting an answer. He peered through the letter-box, then in at the downstairs front window. What he saw there made him grab Vic by the arm to force her to look through the window as well. Then he picked up a large stone from the garden and used it to smash a hole in the glass panel of the front door. This enabled him to reach his arm in through the hole and release the lock so that the pair of them could enter the house.

'What did I tell you? They're burglars all right!' crowed Jack.

'Well, it's a good thing we hung around for proper proof.'

'It's still our word against theirs, and who's going to believe two kids? Pity we didn't have a camera. We should clear off while we still have the chance.'

'Let's just see what they're going to steal, then we can report it.'

While the children were still arguing about what to do next Baz reappeared, leapt into the van and drove away at speed, leaving Vic behind in the house.

'Hey, did you see his hands?' Jack gasped and turned pale with horror. 'They were covered in blood!'

'Now we've *got* to tell somebody!'

'Who, for instance? There's not a soul in sight.'

'Yes, there is! Over there, look! Coming along that path through the trees.'

Jack looked where Sam was pointing, and sure enough there was a figure walking towards them. In the middle of all this villainy would it be someone they could trust?

7
A Bloodthirsty Tale

The approaching figure proved to be that of a girl. Sam thought something about that girl seemed familiar. First it was the way she walked, then as she drew nearer it was her hair, and finally her face.

'Amanda?' Sam cried, running towards the girl in amazed recognition.

'Hi, Sam!' The girl was equally astonished. 'I thought you weren't coming until tomorrow? Couldn't wait, eh?'

'You mean – this is where you live?'

'Sure! I gave you my address, didn't I?'

'Yes, but I didn't know where it was. My mum was going to bring me in the car but then she found she couldn't.'

'Well, if you've come on the bus you got off at the wrong stop. My house is a mile further up the road. There's a stop right outside our gate.'

'No, we didn't come on the bus; it's a long story. We're here by accident, Jack and me.'

Sam introduced her friend and without further ado Jack blurted out their tale. They had been driven here by villains who were actually burgling the house opposite at this

very moment and had probably killed somebody in the process.

Amanda looked really alarmed.

'That's Mrs Pickering's house. She's a
friend of ours, an old lady who lives alone.
My mum sometimes calls on her to see if
she wants any shopping.'

She started towards the house in a panic,
but Jack dragged her back.

'You can't go in there now. One of them's
still there, and the other could drive back at
any minute. Best thing we can do is tell the
police. Where's the nearest phone box?'

Amanda looked stunned for a second,
then she remembered a telephone box a
little way up the road.

'Come on, then! What are we waiting for?'

Keeping to the shelter of the trees, the
children ran as fast as they could in the
direction Amanda showed them. Once they
were well past the house it seemed safe to
emerge on to the road, which meant they
could move faster. All three of them were
hot and breathless by the time the telephone
box came into view. Jack was ahead, already

working out what he would say when he dialled the emergency number.

Then he hit a snag. There was someone already in the telephone box. It was a man standing with his back to Jack, but surely he'd hand over the receiver when Jack explained what had happened?

Jack had already seized the door-handle when the man swung round, scowling at this intrusion.

It was Baz!

8
Dark Suspicions

Back in Seathorpe, Constable Lewis paid a visit to Mrs Cronin, holding in his arms the injured Cameron whom he had found cowering on the grassy verge of a lay-by, near a set of deep tyre-marks.

Mrs Cronin was overjoyed. She received the injured animal tenderly, remarking, with a tear in her eye, how kind someone had been to bandage up his injured paw.

'That's what puzzles me,' the constable pondered. 'Why would anyone go to the trouble of caring for the animal, and then abandon him in a place where he might never be found?'

'Maybe he got away on his own.'

'But he can't walk. He was lying helpless in the long grass, and I'd never have spotted him at all if it hadn't been for this.' The constable took from his pocket a mouth-organ which he had picked up from the same spot.

'It was the sun gleaming on the metal that caught my eye. Then when I bent down to pick it up I heard your Cameron whimper.'

'Why, that's young Jack Butler's har-

monica!' cried Mrs Cronin. Her husband was always telling her how Jack screeched out weird so-called tunes on the instrument in the school yard every chance he got. Once he'd even been caught practising scales in the school boiler-house, setting up a weird accompaniment of knocking in the pipes. Mr Cronin reckoned those pipes had never been the same since.

'Funnily enough, Jack was here a little while ago, him and that Platt girl, trying to tell me that someone was going to break in to the school. Fat chance of that with this new alarm system! I told them about Cammy and they promised to go looking for him, so if they got that close to him why didn't they bring him home, or at least come and tell me where he was? They're good kids really, and they're very fond of our Cammy, as all the children are. They wouldn't have left him lying there on his own.'

Constable Lewis began to look very thoughtful. Was there some connection between the injured dog, the lost mouth-organ, the deep tyre-tracks and Jack's strange rumour? He decided to take the mouth-organ round to Jack's house at once and ask further questions.

It was Mrs Butler who answered his knock.

'Yes, that's our Jack's mouth-organ all right; his dad bought it for him a couple of Christmases ago. Pity you had to go and find it,' she snapped. 'But our Jack's not in. Didn't come home for his lunch. Said he was going to Samantha Platt's, but he never turned up there, and she's not in either because I rang to check. They've run off somewhere to tease us, and that lad's in big trouble when he gets home, you mark my words!'

Upon further questioning, Mrs Butler admitted that the children had each had what she described as 'a bit of a row' at home that morning.

'Mrs Platt told me their Samantha had been ever so cheeky, same as our Jack. Kids! They just ask to get told off, then they go into fits of sulks and try to punish us by pretending to disappear. And of course when two of 'em get together you can expect more than twice the trouble. Anyway, I'm sure you've got better things to do than bothering your head about those two. They'll come home soon enough when they get really hungry.'

Constable Lewis asked what the rows had been about, but Mrs Butler assured him it was all 'something and nothing'. It boiled down to kids not listening. Jack had been told to change his tee-shirt but he reckoned he hadn't heard, then got very cheeky about it. As for Samantha, she'd been told she couldn't go to her friend's house but she wouldn't listen to reasons why, and flounced off in a temper.

What friend was that? the constable wanted to know, but Mrs Butler couldn't tell him. Somebody new, she thought; somebody who lived a long way off, which was why Sam wasn't allowed to go, and quite right too.

Not wishing to alarm Mrs Butler, the constable didn't mention the injured dog, nor hint that he was taking this disappearance more seriously. Yet his next stop was the Platts' house where he did finally manage to obtain Amanda's address from Sam's mother.

'Do you think Samantha and Jack might have gone there by themselves?' he asked her.

'Not a chance!' Mrs Platt assured him.

'For a start, they'd never make it. It's nearly twenty miles away and they don't even know how to get there. I was going to take Sam in the car and it's right out in the country; not an easy place to find. Besides, Billy said no, and our Sam wouldn't dare to disobey Billy.'

The constable was not convinced. Disobedience of one sort or another was something he came across every day of his working life. And since the only crime now outstanding on his patch was a missing broom, he decided to drive out in the direction of Amanda's house, just in case. Perhaps he'd catch up with the children trying to walk there or (much more worrying!) trying to hitch a lift. Then again, maybe young Jack was right and there were burglars about after all. If there were, it certainly wouldn't do for a couple of kids to be chasing them. That was *his* job, and a nice change it would be to get his teeth into a real bit of villainy for a change.

9
A Lucky Meeting

The minute Jack recognised Baz, he swung away from the telephone box but he wasn't quite quick enough. Baz caught him by the arm.

'It's out of order,' sneered Baz disgustedly, letting the broken receiver slip from his bloodstained hand. 'So you're going to have to help me. Do you live round here?'

'No, he doesn't, but I do!' cried Amanda, hurrying to the rescue. 'And I can soon fetch my dad and two big brothers, so you'd better let him go.'

Ignoring this threat, Baz explained that he needed a telephone urgently. He had to get help for an old lady lying injured in a

house down the road. He thought she must have fallen down stairs. There was no telephone in her house, so Baz had driven up here to ring for the ambulance, but vandals had obviously got to the telephone before him.

'But – that's Mrs Pickering!' cried Amanda, appalled at the thought of the old lady's injuries. 'We can ring from our house; it's not far away.'

'Into my van then, all of you! No time to lose!'

'Not likely!' cried Jack. Nothing would induce him to enter that van again.

'We don't take lifts from strangers,' Sam told him. Especially burglars and possible murderers, she added silently.

Amanda explained that there was a short cut to her house through the woods which was much quicker than driving by road.

'Won't be long!' she cried, leading her friends off at the double into the trees before Baz could protest.

'I bet *he* was the one who wrecked the phone, so nobody could set the police on to

71

them,' guessed Jack.

'Or else he was ringing an accomplice and just wanted to get rid of us.'

'No; he wouldn't have let us get away to go and tell the police.'

'Do you think he's killed her?'

'Save your breath for running,' panted Amanda. 'We'll have to get back on the road quite soon, then we'll really have to move! But with any luck he won't be looking. He'll think we're still in the woods.'

'What if he's following us right now?' Sam wondered.

But Jack was thinking that Baz wouldn't risk going near Amanda's house to face her dad and two big brothers. Little did he know that Amanda had no brothers, and her dad was working miles away. Even her mother had gone to see a friend so the house was empty. Amanda had a key on a string round her neck, and a good line in bluff.

'He'll probably drive straight back to Mrs Pickering's to collect Vic,' decided Jack. 'She'll have been packing up the loot.'

'Well, I just hope we can get help quick

enough to catch them before they hop it.'

'And save Mrs Pickering.'

As it turned out, the children need not have worried. For soon after they regained the road a police car pulled up beside them. The man in the driving seat was Constable Lewis.

10
Things Are Not Always What They Seem

Constable Lewis's car, with the three children piled in the back, screeched to a halt behind the white van parked in front of Mrs Pickering's house. The constable had called the emergency services on his mobile phone and an ambulance was already on its way, plus police reinforcements. Ordering the children to stay in the car, he himself leapt out and hammered on Mrs Pickering's front door.

'Police! Open up!'

He was let in by Vic, who seemed relieved to see him.

'That was quick!' she cried, stepping back to allow the constable to pass. 'I'm so glad to see you! We didn't know what to do for the best.'

The old lady called Mrs Pickering was lying unconscious at the foot of the stairs with her head in a large pool of blood.

'That's how she was when we found her.

We daren't move her,' Vic explained.

'No, quite right!' agreed the constable, kneeling beside the old lady and thankfully finding a pulse. 'The paramedics will be here in a minute.'

Suddenly Baz appeared from the kitchen, drying his hands.

'You should make sure your public telephones are in order,' he told the constable. 'It could make all the difference between life and death.'

Constable Lewis explained that this wasn't his patch; he had just happened to be passing. But he promised to mention the matter to the local officer when he turned up.

'Now, sir, if you'll just put me in the picture. How did you get into the house in the first place?'

'We broke in,' Baz admitted. 'We rang the bell, but when there was no answer we looked through the window. We had an appointment, you see, so we knew the old lady must be in.'

'We were a bit late,' added Vic, 'because

we stopped to look after an injured dog we found, but we felt sure she would have waited for us. Then we saw her lying at the foot of the stairs. So Baz picked up a stone and smashed the glass in the door. We'll pay for any repairs, of course.'

'You found a dog?' Constable Lewis was beginning to put two and two together but couldn't quite decide how many they added up to.

'Yes,' agreed Baz, 'it was lying by the roadside and had probably been hit by a car. We thought it belonged to a farm near where we found it. Smart's farm, I believe. We wasted some time plodding up there through a sea of mud to enquire, but there didn't seem to be anyone about.'

'By the time we got back from the farm the dog had vanished,' added Vic. 'We never did work out how it got away.'

Well, that was obviously Cameron, thought the constable, who was beginning to believe that these two were not villains after all. He should have known better than to listen to a bunch of kids. What a yarn they'd spun him in that car! Dognapping, burglary and murder, indeed!

'Are you the old lady's relatives?'

Vic explained that they had never met her before, but had come in answer to an advertisement. They wanted to buy the old lady's computer.

Now, wait a minute! That did seem odd. Mrs Pickering didn't look at all like the sort of person to own a computer. But truth can be stranger than fiction. It turned out that Mrs Pickering's nephew had recently emigrated to New Zealand, leaving various items behind for his aunt to sell. One of these items was a computer, which Baz had wanted his wife Vic to buy.

Vic was a teacher, very unsure of herself in the world of computers, but Baz had finally persuaded her that possessing her own machine was her best way to break in to the new technology while the school was on holiday.

'Hands on; that's what you need!'

He promised he would help her to get to grips with it, so that by the time term started she would be as proficient as the rest of her class.

'It was a lucky advert for the old lady,' added Vic, 'because if we hadn't turned up and discovered her she might have lain there for days. She might even have died. But here's the ambulance now.'

It was late afternoon by the time Constable Lewis drove the children home. First he dropped Amanda at her house. Mrs Ross was home by then, and produced some welcome refreshments. She quite took to Jack and Sam, thinking they would be good companions for Amanda who didn't have many friends nearby. She offered to fetch them in her car to spend a day with Amanda later in the week. In fact, they could come every week during the holidays if they wanted.

'If I fetch you myself, your parents won't have to worry about the journey,' she said after hearing Sam's lament.

'Billy's not my parent,' muttered Sam. But she was delighted to realise that Billy would have to give in gracefully when Mrs Ross

went to all the trouble of collecting them. In fact, she was already looking forward to seeing Billy's face when Amanda's mum turned up at the door. Besides, the school computer was now safe. Life was improving by the minute!

As for Jack, he was bound to admit that he had got hold of the wrong ends of several sticks, just as Constable Lewis had predicted.

That's what comes of listening! he thought disgustedly. Even so, his mum would no doubt go on complaining that he never listened. Well, in future she'd be one hundred per cent right. Because from now on, from this very moment, Jack Butler resolved that, apart from his friends, the only thing he would listen to for the whole of his life would be the telly, his Walkman or his own mouthorgan.

'What about school?' asked Sam. But her question went in at one ear and out at the other.

DANNY –
Don't Jump!

Andersen Young Readers' Library

Hazel Townson

DANNY –
Don't Jump!

Illustrated by Amelia Rosato

Andersen Press · London

For Jack, Lucille and John Littlewood of St. Helier

Contents

I
Creation

First there was the business of the cloakroom washbowl. All Danny did was to drop a football boot into it,
quite accidentally. He never meant to cause a hundred
pounds' worth of damage, and privately thought the
washbowl must have been faulty to start with. Then
there was the newly-planted sapling he walked into
when he was seeing what it was like to be blind, and the
pile of dirty plates that slid from his monitoring hands
halfway through the second sitting of school dinner.
(Well, *that* could have happened to anyone, and if folks
would go leaving slippery lumps of gristle skidding
about in gravy-puddles on every plate, then what
could they expect?) But the fact was that by the time
Danny broke the headmaster's window—and the
Grecian vase that sat on the window-sill—he had
already acquired a reputation, deserved or not, as a
reckless vandal.

'I fail to understand,' said the headmaster, Mr
Cropper, 'how you came to be hurling a Bible across
the playground in the first place.'

Danny thought a man in Mr Cropper's position had

no business to fail to understand, especially when Danny himself had just explained that he had been late for assembly, where he was due to read out a psalm, and had slipped on the core of Reg Hopkinson's apple, which wasn't supposed to have been eaten until lunchtime anyway.

Mr Cropper frowned at Danny over his half-spectacles.

'Well, Danny, I must say I'm disappointed in you. I thought you had the makings of a first-rate sensible lad, but just lately you seem to have run completely off the rails. I think it's high time you turned over not so much a new leaf as a whole new plantation. In this school we're aiming for creation, not destruction. Bear that in mind. See if you can't manage to make some positive contribution . . . .'

Mr Cropper rambled on, but Danny had ceased to listen. The word 'creation' had caught on a hook in his mind, and his whole attention was bent on trying to shake it free.

Danny Lyndon really wanted to be liked, and to live up to other people's expectations. To this end he had suffered many things, such as doggedly learning to swim when he hated the water, sharing his crisps when he was ravenous and putting his precious limbs in the paths of lethal cricket balls. All of a sudden, it seemed, he had become unpopular by accident, and he found

that he wanted to set this right. Creation, eh? Some positive contribution? Well, at least he could start by repairing the Grecian vase with his new tube of Super-glue. He would ask for the pieces at once.

'Sir! If you'll let me—!'

'No more excuses, Danny, please. Your ingenuity has already been stretched to the limit.'

'But if you'll just give me . . . .'

'Least said, soonest mended!' Mr Cropper clapped a monstrously heavy hand on to Danny's shoulder. 'Just remember, boy—actions speak louder than words.'

Well, thought Danny, that was true enough; that last slap of the Cropper's had shouted and screamed all the way through Danny's nervous system. The bell's deafening clang now added to the agony and Danny had to go, casting wistful backward glances at the Cropper's wastepaper basket, wherein reposed the shattered ornament.

Never mind; today was Friday. The Cropper went home promptly on Fridays because of his local history meeting, so Danny would sneak back after school and help himself to the broken bits of vase. What a lovely surprise for the Cropper when he got it back good as new on Monday morning!

At four o'clock Danny sneaked back all right, but he had reckoned without Mrs Bodge, who was busy cleaning the headmaster's office.

'What you doin' 'ere, then?' Mrs Bodge instantly smelled a rat. 'Come for a canin', have you? Well, he's gone, so happen it's your lucky day.'

Danny shook his head. 'They're not allowed to cane us any more. They have to forgive us, which is worse. They go on and on and *on*.' Danny proceeded to explain his errand.

'Broke his window and vase with a Bible, eh? Take a real Christian to forgive that!' Mrs Bodge began to chuckle, remembering that Mr Cropper went to yoga classes; he was probably a heathen.

'I *would* like to have a go at mending it.'

Danny edged towards the basket, looking so wistfully woebegone that Mrs Bodge took pity on him. Riffling through the basket, she picked out the vase bits and set them down on the Cropper's desk.

'There you are, then, and I wish you joy of it. Proper jig-saw puzzle that's going to be. Still, I saw one in a museum once, made up from a hundred and eighty pieces, and you'd never have known except it looked as though it was wearing a hairnet.'

'Thanks, Mrs Bodge!' Danny had dropped the pieces—(luckily there were only seven)—into a cast-off envelope from the same basket, and was heading for the door.

'And don't make an 'abit of it!' Mrs Bodge called after him.

At home, Danny spread out his seven pottery pieces on a sheet of newspaper on the kitchen table and carefully unscrewed the top of his Superglue. He began to stir the pieces around into some sort of shape.

'Oooh, that looks interesting! What is it?' asked Mrs Lyndon, who liked to think of herself as a caring mother.

'It's—er—a project. For art.'

'Well, I never! The things they think of at that school! There was none of that in our day, I can tell you! Proper boring old lessons we had. No chance to develop our artistic talents. You don't know how lucky you are!'

'Yes, I do. But don't stand watching, Mum. You'll make me nervous.'

'Go on with you! You're not nervous of *me*!' cried Mrs Lyndon playfully. 'I wouldn't care if I was always nagging you about dropping glue on the table and sticking your fingers together. I *trust* you. Anyway, you haven't told me what it is yet.'

'It's a Grecian vase.'

'Fancy! A sort of kit, is it? Like those pictures they paint by numbers? Well, you make a good job of it, son—(as I'm sure you will)—and you can put it on the mantelpiece in the front room.'

'I can't keep it, Mum. It's for school.'

'Well, surely they'll let you buy it when you've put all that work into it. They used to do that with our sewing and your dad's woodwork. I'll drop a line to Mr Cropper if you like, and ask him.'

'No, Mum!'

Fortunately, Danny's dad came home just then, and Mrs Lyndon bustled off to see to the dinner. Danny heaved a sigh of relief—but it didn't last long. He suddenly discovered that one piece of the vase—a vital bottom bit—was missing. What a rotten shame, just as he'd started to make the whole thing look quite presentable again! You'd think fate would help out a bit when you were trying to make amends. Well, that left Danny

97

two alternatives. He could throw the whole thing into the dustbin and continue his life of shameful notoriety. Or he could go back to school and hunt for the missing piece. Maybe Mrs Bodge would still be there.

Sneaking off quietly, Danny ran all the way back to school, but he did remember to put the top back on his Superglue first.

2

Destruction

Alas! Mrs Bodge and her cronies had gone; that was the first thing Danny discovered. The whole place was locked up and there wasn't a soul about. The second thing he discovered was that the broken pane in the Cropper's window hadn't yet been replaced. The gap was covered with a sheet of thin plywood, which should not be too difficult to remove. In fact, it proved amazingly easy, as though someone had already had a go at it. A few minutes later Danny, feeling like the worst kind of criminal, yet mystifyingly pleased with himself all the same, was standing in the middle of the Cropper's office, having sellotaped the plywood back into place lest some passing nosey-parker should spot the gap.

So far, so good. Now all he had to do was to find the missing bit of vase. He dropped down on to his hands and knees and started a tour of the carpet, peering under desk and chairs, along bottom shelves and round the backs of cupboards. He did not find what he was looking for. Instead, he caught his foot in the telephone flex and dragged the telephone from the desk to the floor with a resounding clang. Immediately a flock of papers rose from the desk like great, white seabirds disturbed from their private cliff. Ominously they swerved and soared and settled all around the room. Danny crouched motionless, shielding his face in horror. Could they have been exam papers, placed in order of merit? Then, suddenly frantic with panic, Danny leapt to his feet and started chasing the bits of paper. One sheet tore as he tried to snatch it from under his foot, and another sheet managed to slip down behind the radiator where no human hand could follow.

It was whilst he was poking about behind the radiator with the Cropper's long, steel paper-knife that he stabbed clean through the lump of 'Plumber's Mate' gunge with which the caretaker had successfully stopped a recent leak. Water began to drip on to the carpet, then to run out at a faster rate, until a sizeable puddle collected.

How cruel Fate could be! From one small good intention the situation had grown into a hideous nightmare wherein Danny, in true nightmare fashion, found his thinking and his action paralysed. He did not know how long he sat there, gazing at the spreading patch of wet which began to lick the edges of more papers. But at last he roused himself and flew off to the kitchen for a mop.

Gone was the moment when Danny might have retreated and given up the struggle to make amends. Now he was so heavily involved in catastrophe that he simply had to put things right. But where was the mop? He had seen a dinner-lady using it that very day, to stem a river of watery custard flowing down the dining-room's centre aisle. But what had she done with that mop afterwards? Danny flung open all the cupboard doors in sight. He even looked in the fridge, reminding himself painfully of his missed meal. At last he remembered the broom-cupboard next to the kitchen door. He opened the broom-cupboard—and a body fell out.

'I can't think what's happened to our Danny,' said Mrs Lyndon, dishing up mounds of mashed potato. 'I never heard him go out, did you?'

'He'll be here as soon as he smells that dinner,' replied Mr Lyndon confidently. 'Never known him miss a meal.'

'If he's gone further than the gate he won't be *able* to smell it.'

'Well, stick his plate back in the oven. I don't see why we should wait. He knows the meal-times and he has a perfectly good watch.'

'It will all dry up in the oven.'

'Teach him the value of punctuality, then, won't it?'

Mrs Lyndon sighed. 'Here, you start your dinner,

then. I'll just give him a shout.'

She went to the front door and called her son's name. There being no reply, she walked down the path to the gate, then called again.

Esmée Bates, who was swinging on next door's gate, said: 'Your Danny's gone back to school.'

'At this time? Whatever for?'

Esmée shrugged and continued swinging.

'He went up School Lane. Nothing else up there that I know of.' Esmée was not quite as unobservant as she looked, though twice as cheeky.

'Well, if you see him, tell him his dinner's ready.'

Mrs Lyndon was not alarmed. She was even trying hard not to be annoyed. Perhaps Danny had forgotten something? A bit of his project, maybe? If he had gone back to school, no possible harm could come to him there. In fact, it was quite heartening, really, to think the lad was so keen on the place.

Having left school early that Friday, Mr Cropper drove first to the barber's, then home for his evening meal. After watching the teatime news on television, he showered and changed, then started packing his briefcase with the papers he needed for the local history meeting. It was his turn to speak tonight, and he had prepared a talk about Keevan Tower, a crumbling local monument about whose origin there was a deal of controversy. The name 'Keevan' was supposed to be a corruption of the French 'Qui vient?' (Who's coming?) but it was Mr Cropper's belief that this Tower had been built, not by the Normans as a Watch Tower, but in 1720 by a gentleman called Sir Cuthbert Keevayne, as a pseudo-Norman folly. Tonight, Mr Cropper intended to spring this information as a surprise upon his colleagues. For evidence, he had made a pile of copies of an ancient plan of the Tower with a quotation underneath it, referring to 'ye incredyble follye of Sir Cuthbt. Keevayne'. He had come across this evidence in an ancient volume dredged up from the back room of the local library, and since the librarian had told him nobody had even looked at the book for eighty years, he felt sure that his information would drop like a bomb-shell. In fact, the Cropper was hoping to make a bit of a name for himself as a local history researcher.

He stretched out a hand across the dressing-table to gather up this vital pile of copies—and encountered an empty space. He had left the dratted things at school!

'Serves you right for using the school photocopier for your private business,' sniffed his wife.

Mr Cropper looked at his watch. 'Never mind; I'll nip in and get them. Where are my school keys?' He calculated that there was half an hour before his meeting was due to start. Just enough time for the run to school, plus all the fiddle of unlocking and re-locking

the building. No time to waste, however. Mr Cropper
jumped into his car, having aimed a brief farewell peck
at his wife's cheek, and set off at once.

He had not gone more than a couple of hundred
metres when he was flagged down by the vicar, who
had just set out on foot for the local history meeting.
(The vicar himself could not afford to run a car, but
had been secretary of the Local History Society for
more years than anyone could remember.)

There was no help for it; Mr Cropper would have to
offer the vicar a lift. He pulled up, forced a smile on to
his face and flung open the passenger door.

"Evening, vicar!'

'Well met, Mr Cropper!' The vicar was beaming all over his face.

'Spot of business to do at school first, I'm afraid. Won't take a minute, though. Hope you won't mind waiting in the car whilst I just dash in and out.'

The vicar said he didn't mind at all, and began settling himself comfortably into his seat, just as Danny Lyndon opened the cupboard door and the body fell out.

3
Co-operation

The 'body' rolled over and sat up. It turned out to be notorious trouble-maker Connie Kellow from the top juniors—(a year ahead of Danny). Connie looked far more angry than dead.

'What—what are you doing here?' breathed Danny, considerably shaken.

'I could ask you the same thing. Proper put the wind up me you did, charging round school at this time of night.'

'I thought you were a blooming corpse.'

'I was hiding from you, if you must know. I thought you were the Cropper.'

'Did you get locked in, or what?'

'Sort of.' Connie eyed Danny warily, wondering how far she could trust him. Not far, she decided. Anybody who came to school in polished shoes and clean shirt, paid his dinner-money first thing Monday morning and never missed assembly must be on Their side. However, when Danny began explaining his own movements, beginning with the morning's Bible mishap, Connie remembered Danny Lyndon's new repu-

tation. Perhaps the lad could be trusted after all . . . up to a point. Especially if Connie could involve him in her own plans, so that he wouldn't ever be able to tell tales. Now, there was an idea!

'Like school, do you?' Connie probed. 'One of these keen types, are you?'

'It's all right.'

'You wouldn't be sorry, though, if a meteor hit it or something, would you?'

Danny shrugged. 'We'd only get sent somewhere else.'

'There's nowhere else round here to send us, now they've closed Norton Lane Primary because of the numbers going down.'

'They'd think of somewhere, don't you worry. They'd put a tent up in the park, or something.'

'Well, that'd make a nice change, at any rate. You ever been to a fire?'

'A bonfire?'

'A building on fire, stupid! A bit of real excitement, that is. Just imagine, great crackling flames and thick black smoke and everybody running about with hoses and stuff, and shouting fit to bust. Have you ever seen one close to?'

Danny's imagination made a different set of connections. Hoses—water—that leak in the Cropper's office! For a moment he'd forgotten all about it!

'Hey, you don't know where the mop is, do you?'

'Yeah, it was digging me in the ribs a minute ago.' Connie tipped her head towards the cupboard she'd just fallen out of. 'But what do you want a mop for? Going to be sick, are you?'

'There's a bit of a crisis on. Grab that bucket, will you, and come and give us a hand?'

Danny seized the mop thankfully and set off up the corridor with it, calling back a garbled explanation as he went. Connie could hardly believe her ears. 'You don't mean there's water all over the place? Oh, flipping heck, everything'll be all damp and soggy.' Connie snatched the king-size box of matches from the waistband of her jeans and hurled it into the broom-cupboard in disgust. Then she picked up the bucket and trailed sulkily after Danny.

Meantime, on a park bench a mile away from school, two furtive-looking characters were holding a guarded conversation.

'This had better be good,' said Biffer Bond. 'I was supposed to be going to see my auntie in hospital, and she's due to leave me all her money.'

'Urgent, I said it was; not good. We've nearly been rumbled.'

'Eh?' Biffer jerked back on the seat as if he had just been given a massive electric shock. 'How come?'

'I was in this pub last night, and this guy called Cropper was rabbiting on to his pal about some boring old local history society,' explained Archie Pell. 'I wasn't really listening, just sort of daydreaming over my pint, when all of a sudden I heard the name Keevan. So of course my ears pricked up and I started taking notice. It seemed there'd been an argument about the history of Keevan Tower, and this Cropper chap, who turned out to be a teacher, had gone to the library and got them to unearth a book from some back room or other, all about Keevan Tower. It's stuff they don't put out on the library shelves, 'cause there's only one copy and it's precious, being local history.'

'Blimey, they don't know *how* precious!'

'Well, this Cropper borrows the book, he says, and finds a load of stuff in it about who built the Tower and how it looked when it was first finished. You're getting my drift, are you?'

Biffer certainly was. He gave an agonised but silent nod.

'Cropper decided to take the book to school today and photocopy the bits he wanted, and although he hadn't realised it, one of those bits he was pointing out showed—wait for it!—a plan of the secret underground passage.'

'But you said nobody knew about that passage. You said after they'd blocked one end up, two hundred

111

years ago, nobody ever went near it again . . . .'

'I know what I said. I was wrong, then, wasn't I?'

'Well, what are we going to *do*?'

'Just let me finish my tale before you go completely bonkers. I followed this Cropper home, didn't I, and hid myself in his privet till the lights went out. Then I tried to break in, but no joy. That house is a lot better guarded than a lion's dinner. Everything locked and bolted, even the bathroom windows. All double-glazed as well, so it was no use hurling bricks. In the end I decided to wait until today and catch him at school.'

'That was a bit of a risk, Archie. Suppose he hadn't of . . . ?'

'Well, he did. And me, I just strolled into school as bold as a bailiff and asked my way to the headmaster's office. (That's who this Cropper had turned out to be, see?) I knew he wasn't there, because I'd just seen him talking to the caretaker in the yard. Sure enough, there on his desk was this book, on top of the pile of copies he'd just made. In and out in two seconds, I was, and here they are in this suitcase, safe and sound. Now we'll have a nice little bonfire, and all will be well again.'

Biffer sagged with relief. 'Great work, Archie. You did a good job there! But let's have a look at that book before you set fire to it. Sounds interesting.'

'I only hope there's no more copies of it left.' Archie handed over a fast-disintegrating volume with the back

completely loose, and Biffer began riffling the pages. 'Yeah—that passage is marked, like you said! That was a narrow squeak, and no mistake!'

'That was the very bit he was copying, as well. He's marked the page. See here . . : ?' Archie's voice suddenly faded as he held out the top sheet of the pile on his lap. He had been stricken dumb with horror. For the drawing on the sheet was not Keevan Tower at all, but some simple geometry problem with a triangle ABC inside a circle O, and all that nonsense.

'What's up?'

Archie groaned. 'I only picked up the wrong pile of papers, didn't I?'

'Well, of all the . . . .'

'How did I know the old fool was going to put his book down on top of the wrong pile?'

'You could have *looked*.'

'Don't you dare say a word! Or *I* shall start by asking where *you* were when I was lying in the prickly privet half the night and risking my neck in the school, and . . . .'

'All right, all right; I got the message. But I suppose it'll be me that has to go back to the school now to change them papers.'

'Too late! Look at the time! School's closed long since, and he'll have taken the papers home with him. In fact, if we don't get a move on, he'll have set off for his local history meeting as well.' One agonising thought after another fled through Archie's mind. 'We've gotta stop him, Biffer. Come doom or death, we've gotta grab them papers before he starts dishing 'em out to all and sundry.'

'You're telling me!' agreed Biffer, picturing the twenty thousand packets of cigarettes from the hijacked lorry that were neatly piled in that underground passage. If the local history society started poking about down there it would be doom or death all right.

'Well, what are we waiting for? Where does this Cropper geezer live?'

4

Consternation

'I can't understand it,' Mr Lyndon declared. 'What the dickens has our Danny gone back to school for on a Friday night?'

'Maybe he forgot something. He was doing an art project, all bits and pieces. Easy enough to leave one bit behind.'

'Sounds very fishy to me. Didn't it strike you that he can't get back into school at this time of day? There'll be nobody there. You're too easy-going with that lad, letting him wander off just when he feels like it.'

'Oh, go on, blame me! I didn't even know he'd gone. Anyway, he was here when you came in, so you had just as much chance to notice him sneaking off as I had.'

'If it was something genuine he'd have told us. So he must be up to some mischief or other.'

'Why have you started thinking the worst of the lad lately? You don't give him a chance. He's a good lad, our Danny is. Look how he's tidied up and put the top back on his Superglue!'

'Oh yes, he's a good lad all right! That's why we just

had a bill for a new school washbasin, and all those cryptic remarks last parents' evening about trampled trees and shattered dinner plates.'

'They weren't our Danny's fault, any of those things. He told me all about them, and I believed him. They were accidents, pure and simple. Accidents can happen to anybody!'

As she said this, Mrs Lyndon suddenly clapped a hand to her mouth. Suppose Danny had had an accident just now? Suppose he'd slipped and broken his leg, or cut his head open on that nasty wall at the end of the school playground? Or even worse, suppose some kidnapper had waylaid him halfway up School Lane,

which was always deserted on a Friday night? There were some very funny characters about these days.

'Fred, what if he's in trouble? He *has* been away a long time. I think maybe you ought to go and look for him.'

'He *is* in trouble,' Fred retorted grimly.

'No, I mean hurt.' Mrs Lyndon began twisting her hands nervously together. 'You could just have a walk up to school; it wouldn't take you long. In fact, I'll come with you.'

'No; if I have to go I'll go by myself. You stop here in case he comes back. I'll find him—but I warn you, I'll deal with him properly when I do, make no mistake about that. Worrying us out of our wits!' Mr Lyndon began putting his shoes back on and buttoning up his jacket. 'We've put a lot of hard work into bringing that lad up properly. He's not going to spoil it now. A firm hand, that's what he needs while he's going through this funny phase.'

'What funny phase?' Mrs Lyndon was nearly in tears by now. 'I don't know how you can say such things! He could be lying hurt somewhere . . . .'

'And if he makes me late for my darts match, he'll be in double trouble.'

'Fred—!' called Mrs Lyndon helplessly as her husband strode off at a cracking pace. She ran up the garden path, hoping to smooth him down before it was too late. 'Don't go off in such a fury! You'll only regret it!' But Fred was already turning the corner at the top of the road.

Esmée Bates, still swinging on next door's gate, looked on with interest. 'Hey, are you and Mr Lyndon going to get divorced?' she asked with relish.

'What a blooming mess!' Connie Kellow stared enviously at the ruin of the Cropper's office. She felt quite jealous that a soft-looking lad like Danny Lyndon could have achieved nearly as much destruction in a few careless moments as Connie herself had been planning and dreaming of for weeks.

'Well, don't just stand there! Help me mop up.'

Danny was already on his knees, soaking up water as fast with his trouser-legs as with the mop. Now that he was no longer alone, Danny's panic had subsided and in fact he was beginning to experience a fine clearheadedness he had never known he possessed. Certain facts had fallen neatly into place. Connie Kellow, as well as Danny, must have climbed in through that boarded-up window, and Connie was obviously up to no good. Danny had practically caught her red-handed at something or other. Danny was beginning to feel the stirrings of power.

'How about picking those papers up and spreading them out to dry on the window-sill?'

Connie glanced up, ready with a cheeky retort, then changed her mind and did as Danny suggested. If she helped him, he'd be all the more likely to help her later on. And you never knew, if he turned out to be not quite as soft as she'd thought they might even make a team.

It was whilst Connie was dealing with the papers that she happened to glance up through the remaining window-pane—and spotted the Cropper's car turning into the far end of School Lane!

Connie said several unprintable words, two of which Danny had never heard before, then she grabbed Danny's arm and started dragging him towards the door.

'It's him! Can't let *him* in now!' ('Rotten spoilsport,' Connie was thinking, 'turning up here before I've even had a go!')

'Who—the Cropper? We're done for, then. He's got keys, so how can we keep him out?'

'We'll have to barricade the front door.'

'What with?' demanded Danny reasonably as Connie pulled him along the corridor.

'There's that big, heavy table in the entrance hall, and that great bronze bust of the idiot who opened the school. Then there's the P.E. benches, and the stuff from the office—computers and that . . . .'

'We'll never do it in time?' Yet Danny was even

119

more anxious than Connie to keep the Cropper out. He summoned up every last bit of his energy as the two of them began heaving at the great oak table. It was lucky for them that the Cropper had to fiddle with the padlock on the gate—(which both children had, of course, climbed over)—for this took up another precious few minutes, by which time the barricade was mounted. Connie Kellow had certainly proved herself as tough as any boy.

'There are all the other doors as well,' panted Danny, but Connie reminded him that all the other doors were bolted on the inside; only the front door could be opened with keys. That was a relief of sorts, but Danny immediately began to worry that the front-door barricade would never hold.

'Yeah, 'course it'll hold against a weedy old stick like the Cropper. Don't know what we'll do if he fetches the Law, though. A couple of burly constables would soon shift it.'

Danny hadn't thought of that. He didn't fancy the idea of the Law at all. In fact, it filled him with fresh panic. How had he got into this mess? Up to now, he had been a law-abiding citizen with a grudging respect for authority. He could just imagine his dad's reaction if asked to turn up at some police station to bail out his only son.

'Can't we undo the bolts and nip out the back?'

'Not likely! The Cropper would be sure to see us if we ran off now.'

'Well, let's get back in the broom-cupboard.'

'What, both of us? You must be joking! I nearly suffocated in there on my own. Besides, he'll know we're here because of the barricade, so if he gets in he'll look everwhere till he finds us, broom-cupboard and all.'

Danny turned pale, and for a moment he thought he really was going to be sick. What a final indignity, in front of Connie Kellow!

'Tell you what, though,' Connie suddenly suggested: 'We could get up on to the roof through that trap-door in the cloakroom ceiling.'

This was not such a wild suggestion as it might have seemed, for the school roof was flat, and Connie had often sneaked up there for an illicit spot of sunbathing in the summer holidays.

'The Cropper would see us on the roof all right.'

'Not him! There's that great big ledge all round. We could easy duck down behind that and wait till he'd gone.'

It was worth a try. They could already hear the Cropper rattling at the door and cursing in a most un-headmaster-like fashion. He must already have real-ised what had happened.

The two of them charged along to the cloakroom,

where they knew that the caretaker's ladder lay neatly along the floor behind the heating pipes. It was tied to those pipes with ropes, and every child was forbidden to touch that ladder on pain of instant expulsion. In no time, Connie and Danny had the knots untied and the ladder set up, though there was one heart-stopping moment when the rising ladder demolished the cloakroom light-bulb with a sound sufficient to rouse the Pharaohs.

'I'll go first,' offered Danny, more out of fear than bravery. He didn't like heights, and had once had to turn shamefully back when halfway up a lighthouse's spiral stair. He must tackle that ladder now, at once, before he had time to think. And indeed, it turned out to be surprising what you could do when death and destruction seemed to be battering at the door. Danny shot up that ladder like the temperature of an Eskimo newly arrived at the equator.

'Watch what you're doing, you nutcase!' Connie yelled as the ladder jumped and shuddered. She threw her weight against the bottom, to hold it steady, but as Danny leapt frenziedly from the top step to the safety of the upper floor, the ladder swung outwards under his final kick, then fell away in splendid slow motion, hanging for a moment in mid-air, completely unsupported, before it fell with a crash right on top of Connie Kellow.

5
Distraction

'Yes?' frowned Mrs Cropper, answering the urgently-ringing doorbell. There were two very odd-looking men on the doorstep, and her first thought was that they had come to offer to clean the drains.

'Is Mr Cropper in? We have to see him urgent,' Archie Pell announced.

'Oh—you've just missed him, actually. He's gone off to his local history society meeting.'

Mrs Cropper was about to shut the door again, but Biffer Bond had slipped his foot into the gap. 'Now, that's a pity. We'll have to go and catch him up. Where would this meeting be?'

By now Mrs Cropper had decided that she didn't like the look of these two at all. They might be planning to mug her husband, or something even worse. So she lied with commendable presence of mind—(as indeed she did whenever an irate parent turned up on the doorstep)—'I don't know where he is tonight. They choose a different meeting-place every week.'

'I wonder why they do that?' Archie began to think this local history society might not be as innocent as it

seemed. He took a thoughtful step forward as he spoke, and Mrs Cropper, in turn, retreated a step away from him. Before she realised what had happened, the two men were in the hall and the front door had closed behind them.

'There's no need to be nervous,' smiled Archie like a hungry crocodile. 'All we want to do is to join the local history society.'

'Yeah, we're great joiners, we are,' Biffer agreed, enthusiastically sawing the air with his heavily be-ringed right hand.

'Tell you what, if you can find us the telephone

number of the meeting-place as well as the address, we'll just have a quick word with your husband and tell him we're coming along, seeing we've left it so late. Don't want them to start without us.'

'I've *told* you, I know nothing about the meeting-place. And now, if you'll excuse me, I have a huge pile of ironing to get through whilst my husband is out.'

'Just a minute, lady! I don't think you realise how important this meeting is to us. Could be a matter of life and *death*.' Mrs Cropper did not like the way Biffer suddenly began flexing his knuckles. Wild ideas shot through her brain like a speeded-up film.

'Oh—I'll tell you what! I've just had a brainwave! His diary! He might have written the meeting-place down in there. He's very careful and methodical, you know. He writes everything down. I'll—I'll go and fetch it.'

'I'll come and help you,' Archie offered genially, taking another few steps forward. 'Don't want you to waste too much of your ironing time.'

'It's—probably in the kitchen drawer.' Mrs Cropper had some hysterical notion of being able to grab the carving-knife for self-defence—but there was no chance of that with Archie Pell breathing down her neck. Archie followed her closely from table to dresser, and there were sounds of drawers opening and shutting smartly. Of course, the diary was not there; never had been there. (As a matter of fact, Mr Cropper did not even keep a diary, dismissing them as 'schoolboy nonsense'.) They tried the living-room next, then the sitting-room, then Mr Cropper's tiny study which was really supposed to be a breakfast-room. There, at last, Mrs Cropper managed to steal a furtive glance at the clock and was thankful to see how much time had passed since her husband left home. Much more than half an hour. Mr Cropper would be safely at his meeting by now, surrounded by stalwart comrades. Thank goodness! Mrs Cropper had played for time and won. Now she could try a fresh manoeuvre.

'Silly me!' she giggled. 'I've just remembered—the meeting's at school tonight. I can't think how I came to forget! You know where the school is, I'm sure—at the top of School Lane?'

'We know!' Archie assured her disgustedly. Biffer was already making for the door.

Trembling all over, Danny Lyndon peered dizzily down from the trap-door. Was Connie dead? She was lying very still, eyes closed and a trickle of blood starting brightly across her forehead. The fallen ladder lay diagonally across Connie's stomach like a giant crossing-out. Obviously Connie needed instant help, but since the ladder had gone, Danny was trapped up there. Fat lot of help he could be! On top of the guilt and horror, Danny almost wept with frustration. Things went on getting worse and worse. The Cropper's leaking radiator was a Bank Holiday treat, compared to this. Now, Danny was faced with an emergency to end all emergencies—a '999' job, an honest-to-goodness matter of life and death. Whatever state the Cropper's room was in, whatever trouble lay ahead, Danny would have to shout to the head for help. Danny wondered what would happen to him. A long spell in prison, maybe. Well, even that was better than dragging through life with the death of Connie Kellow on his conscience. Blooming marvellous, though! You started out trying to create and make a positive contribution, and you finished up in the middle of a life of crime!

It was no use shouting from the rafters, Danny decided; no one could possibly hear him from there. He would have to venture out on to the roof all on his own. Gingerly, he progressed across the insubstantial floor and began struggling with the bolts on the little door. Finally he got the door open and emerged on to the school's flat roof. But one step more was all he took. Immediately, the lurching sky and swaying chimneys set his stomach churning. He closed his eyes and clung to the door behind him. In his imagination he had already turned giddy and hurtled from the low parapet to the ground below, where he lay splashed like a tomato on a tax-collector's windscreen. But the memory of poor Connie surfaced slowly, and Danny pulled himself together. He opened his eyes again, lowering his gaze to something more solid. That was when he caught sight of the precarious cat-walk round the edge of the roof—nothing more than rotting wooden slats with goodness knew what hazards down between them if your foot should chance to slip. How could he ever dare to walk on those? All the same, something must be done. He took a deep breath, then removed one hand from the door behind him. Next he took one trembling step forward before closing his eyes again. At last, still metres from the edge of the roof, he managed to make some sort of unintelligible croak which he hoped the Cropper would identify as a call for help. But the croak was carried away on the wind. The Cropper, busy battering at the front door with a rapidly-bruising shoulder, did not hear. In any case, he had just decided to go back to his car and consult the vicar.

'Can't get into the school!' Mr Cropper massaged his wounded shoulder. 'Someone's barricaded the door. What the dickens do you make of that?'

'Very odd,' replied the vicar. 'Are you *sure* you can't get in?'

'How could I not be sure? I've been battering the door—and myself—for the last ten minutes. I wouldn't be surprised if I've done myself a permanent injury.'

'Perhaps the lock's jammed. It happens sometimes.'

'Rubbish! Both keys turned, the latch and the mortice, but I couldn't budge the door itself. Either the caretaker's gone mad, or some of the kids are in there, up to no good.'

'Oh, I can't imagine—!'

'Well, I can! If you knew what some of those kids get up to, vicar, you'd be trying to slip your sermons into the *Jackanory* programme. Why, only today, one of 'em flung a Bible through my window.'

'Dear, dear!' The vicar looked shocked. 'What will you do, then?'

'I shall ring the police, that's what. Your phone's probably the nearest. Do you mind . . . ?'

'Don't you think that's a little drastic, fetching the police to such young children?'

'It's a little drastic for me to be shut out of my school! Drastic, and extremely inconvenient. As it is we shall be late for our meeting—if we get there at all!'

'We could come back after the meeting.'

'And find the place vandalised from top to bottom? Fish-tanks overturned, desks upended, rude writing on all the blackboards? No, thank you! Anyway, I want my sheets of paper.'

The Cropper jumped sulkily back into his car, and slammed the door so hard that the handle fell off on the outside.

Halfway down School Lane, Mr Cropper met Mr Lyndon hurrying along on foot. He braked immediately and wound down his window, recognising a conscientious parent when he saw one, for Mr Lyndon never missed a parents' evening or school function, and had once stood in as emergency referee for a football match when half the staff were down with 'flu.

'Anything wrong, Mr Lyndon?' Two and two were already hurling themselves triumphantly together in Mr Cropper's mind.

'Have you got my lad there?' Mr Lyndon tried to peer into the car.

'Danny? Why, no, not at this time of night. Hasn't he been home?'

'In once, then out again. Came back to school. He was seen.'

'Ah! Well, in that case—' Mr Cropper was interrupted by Mrs Lyndon, who now came panting along behind her husband in a state of terrible agitation. Arms waving wildly, she was shouting: 'Get him down! Get him down before he kills himself!'

Sensing tragedy, the vicar leapt out of his side of the car. He and the others stared first at Mrs Lyndon, then at the spot she was pointing to. There, on the roof of the school, they saw the top half of the figure of a small boy, slowly approaching the edge.

'Danny—don't jump!' yelled Mrs Lyndon frantical-

131

ly. Then she broke free from the vicar's restraining arm and chased on towards the school.

6

Conflagration

Soon after Danny had gone, Mrs Bodge had discovered the missing piece of Grecian vase in a geranium-pot which had shared the fateful window-sill. She slipped the fragment into her apron pocket, thinking she might call at Danny's house with it on her way home. He'd been so keen to mend that ornament, bless him! The only snag was, Mrs Bodge didn't know where Danny lived.

'Bound to be some of our kids around, though; I'll ask one of them.'

In fact, Mrs Bodge was sent off—(accidentally or on purpose, she never found out which)—in the wrong direction by a lad called Reg Hopkinson, and it was quite a long time before she decided to give up and go home. Only then, when she was halfway back home, did she come across Esmée Bates, swinging dizzily on a gate.

'Danny Lyndon? Yeah, he lives next door, but he's not in. There's nobody in.'

'Never mind, love; you can give this to Danny for me when he comes back.' Mrs Bodge held out the bit of pottery, but Esmée made no move to take it.

'He isn't coming back. He's run away from home and he's hiding in school. His mum and dad are going to get divorced.'

Good-hearted Mrs Bodge was shocked. 'Oooh, what a terrible thing! I don't know what the world's coming to, honest I don't!' She slipped the bit of pottery back into her pocket and went off in the direction of school, tutting and shaking her head. 'No wonder he threw his Bible, the poor lamb!' Well, the least she could do was to go and see if Danny was all right. Had he had a meal? Where was he going to sleep? And what sort of a state was he in? Why, the lad could do anything if he was that upset! Mrs Bodge discovered that she had quite a soft spot for Danny Lyndon, and quickened her pace.

By the time Mrs Bodge arrived at the school gate, the drama was in full swing, Mrs Lyndon weeping wildly in the vicar's arms, Mr Lyndon halfway up a drainpipe trying to reach the school roof, and Mr Cropper speeding off in his car to summon help.

'Well, I never!' cried Mrs Bodge indignantly to the vicar. 'You, of all people, mixed up in a divorce!'

'I beg your pardon?'

'Right under his nose, too, the poor lamb! Where is he?'

'On—on the r-roof!' sobbed Mrs Lyndon. 'He's

going to jump!'

'I'm not surprised!' Mrs Bodge would have said a great deal more, but at that moment there was a blood-curdling yell from the direction of the school and a sickening thump as Mr Lyndon fell from the drainpipe to the playground. Mrs Bodge could not help a small smile of relief. 'Oh, him! For a minute I thought you meant *Danny* was going to jump!'

Mrs Lyndon and the vicar ran to help up Mr Lyndon, who was not badly hurt. He had grazed his hands, bumped his nose and bruised himself a bit, but there was no cause for alarm. Except that he had now

realised he would not be able to reach his son by way of the drainpipe. That meant he was helpless until Mr Cropper came back with reinforcements.

'Can't we find a ladder, or something?' cried Danny's dad distractedly, dashing off on a fruitless search.

Once Mrs Lyndon was assured her husband was still alive, she returned to the front drive, whence she could keep her son in view and call to him.

'Danny—your dad's all right; he isn't hurt! Hang on a minute, love, we're fetching help. Your dad didn't mind about that hundred pounds, nor the tree and the dinner plates. If he seems a bit cross sometimes, it's just his way. Don't jump, love! Promise Mum you won't jump!'

Danny, who had no intention of jumping, could not make out what his mother was saying. All he knew was that he had been spotted; and he presumed that meant his message about Connie had been received. His knees suddenly felt weak with relief and he sat down, which put him out of sight from the ground.

'He's gone!' screamed Mrs Lyndon, making off round the side of the school. 'He's disappeared! He's going to jump from the other side! Oh, Danny!'

Mrs Bodge, who was beginning to get the hang of things, decided that, as everybody else seemed to be in a flap, she had better take charge of the situation. These three had driven the lad almost to suicide, then lost their nerve. It was up to her, Mrs Bodge, to sort the whole thing out.

Cupping her hands, she called out in her loudest voice: 'Can you hear me, Danny? It's Mrs Bodge, what helped you find them pieces. You'll have noticed there's one missing. Well, I've got it right here in my pocket. You could finish your vase in no time, then think how pleased His Nibs'd be. You don't want to do nothing silly till you've mended that vase, now do you?'

No sign from above, just a nerve-racking silence.

'Well, don't just stand there!' Mrs Bodge nagged the vicar. 'At least you could say a prayer for the lad, or think of a good quotation from the Bible.' She herself drew nearer to the school building, ready to call again, but suddenly became aware of two figures approaching the school. Could this be help? She decided to wait and see.

Archie Pell gave Mrs Bodge a friendly wave as he and Biffer Bond strode purposefully up to her. Was she going to the local history meeting, they asked.

'What, me? You must be joking! Takes me all my time to live one day at once, never mind what's past and done.'

'Well, which room is the meeting in?' asked Biffer.

'No meeting here tonight, that I do know! Though I must say there's plenty of other things going on.'

Whilst this exchange was taking place with Biffer,

Archie had moved up to Mr Cropper's window, which he remembered from his visit earlier in the day. Peering in, he saw the papers Connie had picked up and set to dry on the window-sill. They were the very ones he was looking for—the copies of the plan of Keevan Tower with the secret underground passage clearly marked. He couldn't believe his luck! He pushed at the plywood with a heavy hand, and was even more astonished when it fell easily into the room. Archie leaned in after it.

'Now, there's someone with a bit of sense at last!' cried Mrs Bodge. 'Why didn't I think of that?' She presumed, of course, that Archie was on his way through the window to rescue Danny, and ran up to give instructions: 'Go out of that door, turn left, then left again till you come to the cloakroom. There's a trap-door on to the roof. But be careful what you say; the lad's upset. Coax him, don't bully him.' She was completely flabbergasted when Archie Pell began retreating from the broken window again with his arms full of papers.

The fire-engine came clanging all the way up School Lane, with the Cropper's car following and Esmée Bates and a whole crowd of kids running excitedly behind that. Danny heard the noise and stood up again to see if it really was a fire-engine.

'There he is!' the vicar yelled. 'Now, keep still, Danny my boy, and perhaps if we were to sing a little hymn it would help? What about "All things bright and beautiful"?' In his best Harvest Festival voice, the vicar began to sing, though the sound was completely lost among the sirens and the shouts. Mr and Mrs Lyndon reappeared with more disjointed messages, and the fire-engine swerved to a halt. Immediately a turntable ladder soared into the air, bearing a helmeted fireman up towards the school roof. There was a concerted gasp, then silence. Everybody's head turned upwards.

Yes—no—yes—Danny was safely in the fireman's arms at last! Only then did the tension in the watching crowd relax. Mrs Lyndon broke into sobs and collapsed into her husband's arms, whilst Mrs Bodge was surprised to find two big tears rolling slowly down her cheeks.

'Poor little lamb!' she sniffed to the vicar. 'And after all that, they go and make it up again!'

Wrapped in a blanket, Danny babbled hysterically about some girl lying injured with a ladder on top of her, but when firemen went back on to the roof and down through the trap-door they found no sign of an injured girl. True, there was a ladder, lying where Danny must have let it fall. There was also a quantity of broken glass and a single spot of blood, and in

addition the bolts on the back door were unfastened. But there was no trace of any child but Danny. The firemen concluded that Danny was suffering from shock.

By now, as no mangled bodies were appearing, the crowd of onlookers was beginning to feel disappointed, and in fact one or two had started to drift away, when suddenly Esmée Bates cried joyfully: 'Fire!' Surely enough, there was a thick plume of smoke gliding out through the ventilator in the broom-cupboard next to the school kitchen.

7
Retribution

'Thirty copies he made; I heard him say it, not once but three times over,' Archie Pell told Biffer Bond as they sat in Biffer's lodgings counting the sheets they had rescued from Mr Cropper's office.

'Well, there's only twenty-nine sheets here.'

'We might as well have rescued none as twenty-nine. They can find out about the secret passage just as fast from one copy as from thirty million.' Archie looked exceedingly depressed, but for once in his life Biffer came up with an original idea. 'We could always move the cigarettes,' he said.

'What?' Archie was shocked at first, but slowly a grin began to spread across his face. 'You know, Biffer, I think you've got something there! But where could we move 'em to?'

'What's wrong with here? My landlady's just gone off for a fortnight's holiday. By the time she gets back, we'll have sold the lot—or smoked 'em.' Encouraged by one brainwave, Biffer had another. 'We could hire a van from that garage down the street, and drive up to the Tower first thing in the morning. We could shift 'em all in one journey then.'

'Not till tomorrow morning?'

'Nobody's going to start looking for secret passages at this time of night. It's nearly dark already.'

'Sometimes, Biffer, you amaze me!' Archie slapped his companion heartily on the shoulder, starting off a nasty coughing fit. Biffer doubled up in agony, trying to say something between the gasping, heaving, choking spasms. At last he got it out: 'For Pete's sake— gimme a cigarette!'

'Of all the rotten luck!' sneered Esmée Bates. 'Having a fire-engine right on the spot when your school starts burning down! It never had a chance!' Indeed, the firemen had made short work of the barricade, and the fire in the broom-cupboard, which had been started, they thought, by an exploding box of matches. Mrs Bodge declared that no matches were ever kept in there, which made another mystery to add to the evening's toll.

'Never mind; all's well that ends well,' declared the vicar, but Mr Cropper, making a tour of inspection, was not so sure. Those firemen seemed to have squirted water everywhere, even inside his own room, though it was well removed from the site of the fire. Everything in Mr Cropper's room was damp, and some of his possessions seemed to have been moved about rather a lot. In fact, a few of them were missing, which puzzled him until Mrs Bodge came offering to help, and told him about the two men making off with his papers. (Geometry problems? Who on earth would want those?)

'You know, Mrs Bodge, there have been some funny goings-on at this school tonight, and I don't think we've heard the last of them yet, by any means.'

'But why would anyone want to steal your papers?'

'I don't know yet, but I shall certainly look into it.'

'There's something else you ought to look into, as well. That lad, Danny Lyndon, was ever so upset about your vase. He wanted to find all the bits, so he could glue them together again.'

Mr Cropper looked up sharply. 'Oh, dear! You're not suggesting that was what made him so upset he was going to . . . ?'

'Jump? Well, it might have had something to do with it, but he was really fretting about his mam and dad splitting up.'

'Splitting up? The Lyndons? Why, they're the very last people I would have thought of . . . .' Mr Cropper sat down suddenly. 'This is a night of surprises, and no mistake! So that's why the boy got into his silly phase these last few weeks?'

'Yes, and maybe if you'd all been a bit more under-standing, this would never have happened.'

A mile away, in the hospital waiting-room, Mr and Mrs Lyndon sat drinking cups of tea while Danny underwent a check-up. As the boy was still insisting upon his unlikely tale of the dying girl—(his latest version was that she had burnt up in the fire)—there had been some talk of keeping him in overnight, for observation.

'What on earth possessed the lad?' worried Mr Lyndon. 'Rampaging about on the school roof! I can't understand it!'

'I'm sure there's a perfectly simple explanation,' insisted Mrs Lyndon, 'just as there was about the sink and all those other little accidents.'

'In my experience, the word "accident" is often just an excuse for all sorts of unsavoury goings-on.'

'Well, don't forget the boy's ill. We've got to be very gentle with him.'

Mr Lyndon grunted, tenderly massaging his damaged nose and trying to ease his bruises on the hard wooden bench. If anybody was ill, he felt, it was himself, but of course it would be Danny who got all the sympathy.

Presently a nurse appeared and said that Danny could be taken home. 'I should put him straight to bed, though, without discussing this any more. And let him take things easy tomorrow. He's a bit shaken up and confused.'

Thankfully, the Lyndons collected their child and ordered a taxi to take them home. On the way they tried hard to talk cheerfully of anything but the subject on their minds.

'Well, Danny, your mother tells me you're doing a project for art, then.'

'Am I?'

'Of course you are, dear! You've just forgotten, but never mind.'

'Dad, isn't anybody going to look for Connie Kellow? She could be bleeding to death, or anything.'

'Are you still going on about . . . ?'

'Sssh!' Mrs Lyndon laid a warning finger to her lips. 'Get your key out, Dad, we're nearly home.'

Mr Lyndon felt in his pocket for his front door key. It was not there. He had rushed out in such a hurry to look for Danny that he had forgotten to pick it up. Still, he remembered having told his wife to stay at home, in which case he wouldn't have needed a key. So this was all her fault.

'Have you got *your* key?' he asked Mrs Lyndon. But his wife kept her keys in her handbag, and of course you don't give a thought to accessories when you are chasing your missing son. Her handbag was still on the kitchen dresser.

'Are we locked out?' Danny showed a spark of interest. 'I could climb in through the kitchen window. Mum never shuts it properly.'

'You've done enough climbing for one night. Leave it to your dad.' Mrs Lyndon suddenly had another thought: 'Oh, Fred! Haven't you any money for the taxi, either? We'll have to borrow from Mrs Bates then, but I do hate borrowing.' She jumped crossly from the taxi and laid a hand on the Bateses' garden gate. It promptly fell apart at the hinges, subsiding to the path with a deafening clatter. (So much for Esmée's swinging marathon!) Mrs Lyndon looked shaken and upset, but Danny said, 'Never mind, Mum! It was only an accident.'

Ten minutes later, when Mr Lyndon was halfway through the kitchen window—(and a very tight squeeze he was finding it to be)—he felt an even tighter grip on his ankle and a stern voice called: 'Now then! Let's have you out of there!'

It was the local police constable, newly drafted here from country parts, and anxious to make a good job of his new assignment.

It took red-faced Mr Lyndon quite a time to extricate himself from the window, whereupon he protested that he'd lived in that house for fourteen years.

'That's what they all say,' smirked the constable, pulling out his notebook and pencil.

'But you surely don't think I'm a burglar? There's a perfectly simple explanation. The whole thing's just a little accident.'

The constable grinned. 'In my experience,' he said, 'the word "accident" is often just an excuse for all sorts of unsavoury goings-on.'

8

Exploration

'I didn't start that fire,' said Connie Kellow, meeting Danny at his gate very early the next morning.

'I never said you did.'

'No, I know.'

'How's your head?' Connie had a plaster on her forehead where she had cut it when the ladder fell.

'Oh, it's okay. How's yours?'

'Nothing wrong with my head.'

'I heard you'd been having visions, seeing dead bodies all over the place.'

'Yeah, I need my eyes testing.' Danny began to walk away, having lost interest in Connie now that he knew she was alive and well, but Connie stopped him. 'Hang about a minute! I've got something to show you. That's why I've come round here.' She began unfolding a grubby sheet of paper which she had fished out from behind the radiator in the Cropper's office the previous night.

'See that? It's a plan of Keevan Tower.'

'So?'

'So it's got a secret underground passage. Bet you

never knew.'

'Bet the builders never knew, either.'

'No, honest! Have a proper look!'

Danny looked. 'Huh!' he said at last.

'Suppose we go and sniff it out? Just you and me. Be a good adventure, that would.'

'No, thanks.'

'Scared, are you?'

'Let's just say I don't want to make a fool of myself, looking for something that isn't here.'

'It *says* it's there. Can't you read?'

'Then how come you're the only one that knows about it?'

Connie's lips tightened. 'Okay then, *be* like that! I can find it by myself.' She stuffed the paper into her pocket and walked away whistling.

'Danny!' Mrs Lyndon, still in her dressing-gown, peeped anxiously round the half-open front door. 'You're up early. Are you all right, love? I was going to bring you your breakfast in bed.'

'I'm fine, Mum!' Danny didn't sound it. Had he just let a perfectly good adventure slip through his fingers?

Mrs Lyndon had been going to ask, 'Was that the girl. . .?' but stopped herself just in time. Best not to start Danny off on his fantasies again. In fact, she must try to keep him occupied all day. 'Tell you what, how about coming shopping with me after breakfast? We could buy a new jig-saw puzzle and I'll help you get it started.'

Connie Kellow, never having tried to live up to anybody's expectations except her own, had no difficulty in reaching Keevan Tower very early that Saturday morning, whilst the dew was still deep enough to soak her socks and track-shoes. It was a cool day with a threat of rain, and there was nobody else about; only a self-drive hire van parked behind the Tower. She stood for a while, studying the plan she had found, and looking at the ruin with a new eye. Then she climbed over a tumbledown bit of wall that said DANGER— KEEP OUT and began carefully searching the ground.

Half an hour later, Connie came across a small hole overgrown with creepers. There was a big flat stone nearby, which looked as if it might once have covered the hole, and the creepers could be coaxed aside to reveal a flight of worn steps leading down into the earth. It was all exactly as the notes had described. Fishing out her torch, Connie started carefully downwards and kept on—until she heard muffled voices. She stopped and listened. The voices seemed to be rising from below. Could the place be haunted? There was also an eerie dragging sound—like heavy boxes being pulled along rough ground.

Well, this was a real adventure, all right! Not only was there a proper secret passage, but there was somebody—or something—actually in it! If only that Danny Lyndon hadn't been so soft, she'd have had somebody to share the fun with. ('Have to put new life into him one of these days,' Connie promised herself.)

Bravely, Connie continued her progress. It took her a few more minutes to realise that the voices and dragging sounds were getting nearer. By the time she actually caught sight of the two men, it was far too late to run away.

Danny Lyndon mooched around his back garden, kicking at bits of stone. He was utterly fed up. Since Connie's departure he had had to endure a series of excruciating scenes. First there was his dad, still smarting from his tangle with the Law, trying hard to 'understand', yet obviously resentful at the unfairness of it all, since nobody had understood *him*. Then there was his mother, treating Danny with exaggerated fuss and false jollity, as if he were royalty about to be wrongly beheaded. Worst of all, the Cropper had turned up whilst breakfast was still on the table, and had actually tried to apologise for misunderstanding everything. He had kept on casting meaningful glances, not only at Danny but at his parents too, provoking puzzlement in Mum and further irritation

154

in Dad. All sorts of cryptic remarks fell from the Cropper's lips, yet none of them made sense. It was worse than anything Danny had ever lived through, with the possible exception of the thought that he might have killed Connie Kellow. So what with one thing and another, the whole situation at home just now was unbearable. If this was the result of trying to live up to people's expectations, then the sooner Danny stopped, the better. He would abandon all attempts to please the grown-ups and concentrate on his contemporaries instead. Connie Kellow was the only person today who had treated Danny normally. Perhaps if Danny were to follow Connie up to Keevan Tower after all . . . ?

Danny glanced around. His mother was furtively watching him through a looped-up corner of kitchen curtain. She beamed a great, false smile when she saw she was spotted. Danny gave her a half-hearted wave, then ambled carelessly round to the front of the house—where he caught sight of Mrs Bodge, approaching along the street with a huge bunch of flowers!

That did it! Danny broke into the fastest run of his life. It took him no more than fourteen minutes all the way to Keevan Tower.

He was just in time to see two unsavoury-looking men bundling a struggling, protesting Connie Kellow

into a van and driving away. Danny noted the number
of the van and ran straight home again.

'Connie Kellow's just been kidnapped!'

'Danny, where have you *been*? I thought we told you
not to leave the garden today, except with one of us?
You're supposed to be convalescing. And Mrs Bodge
has come to see you. Look at the lovely flowers!'

Danny spun round and ran off again to find a
policeman.

157

9
Conclusion

On Monday morning, the crowd in the school playground pressed close around its heroine, Connie Kellow. To have been kidnapped by cigarette thieves, then rescued as the thieves were caught, was enough to ensure Connie's glory for the rest of the term. But strangely enough she had turned the focus of attention on to Danny Lyndon.

'As for him, he was scared going up the ladder, and he was scared to look for that underground passage. Left me to catch them cigarette thieves on my own,' she declared, gesturing rudely at Danny who hovered on the edge of the throng.

'Fat lot of good it would have done you if they'd shredded you up for extra tobacco,' Danny pointed out. 'I was the one who set the police after you. If it hadn't been for me . . . .'

'If it hadn't been for you, capering about on the school roof last Friday, the school might have burnt down,' cried Esmée Bates.

'Yeah, trust him to spoil all the fun!'

Danny Lyndon stared at the crowd of faces, turning

now towards him and beginning to look decidedly hostile. 'There's no pleasing some folks!' he said disgustedly. He felt aggrieved that Connie Kellow should be the heroine of the moment, whilst he had had to make do with a series of tickings-off for disobeying various instructions, and being rude to Mrs Bodge. At one point on Saturday, Danny had almost begun to feel that he and Connie had shared an adventure after all; might even share others in the future. But Connie's present betrayal had hurt him badly. She ought to have been grateful for being rescued, but instead of that she'd done her best to belittle his efforts and put him in the wrong.

'You should have seen him at the top of that ladder!' Connie was jeering now. 'I don't know which of them was dithering the most. It could've killed me, that ladder could!'

'Serves you right for breaking into school in the first place!'

'I only went to get my cardigan. Anyway, hark at him! Little Goody Two-Shoes! You know what *he* was up to? He was snooping round the Cropper's desk, looking through all his papers. No wonder he always does so well in the exams!'

'You rotten liar!' Danny Lyndon saw red. He swung his lunch-bag up and lunged at Connie with it. Four salami sandwiches, one banana, one orange and a bag

159

of Chipples would have made quite an impact on Connie's cheeky face. But unfortunately the lunch-bag flew out of his hand and soared across the playground in a wide, impressive arc. Danny closed his eyes. He knew what was going to happen, and it did. There was an ominous tinkling sound, followed by a more substantial crash.

'That's more like it!' Connie Kellow crowed. 'I knew he had it in him!' She set the whole crowd cheering, and led them in a circular war-dance round Danny. Finally, she leapt to Danny's side, winked, held out her hand and grinned. 'Shake!'

All at once, Danny Lyndon realised with amazement that he had achieved his life's ambition. He was popular at last.

ONE GREEN BOTTLE

Andersen Young Readers' Library

HAZEL TOWNSON

ONE GREEN BOTTLE

Illustrated by David McKee

Andersen Press · London

Contents

I

All in the Game

'Why isn't he in the school football team?' Tim Evans's Aunt Maisie asked.

'Why *aren't* you in the school football team?' Tim's mother asked Tim.

'Because I'm not good enough,' said Tim.

'Not good enough?' cried Aunt Maisie indignantly. 'When your Uncle Cyril was Cleckhampton Rovers' goalie for seven years?'

'Of course he's good enough,' retorted Mrs Evans, who was Uncle Cyril's sister. 'He's just lazy, that's all. Won't be bothered to practise.'

'Yes, I will!' protested Tim. 'I mean, I would if I was good enough.'

'Well, you never will be good enough if you don't practise,' said his mother, and there was no answer to that.

Tim Evans had lost another argument. Worse, he had been made to feel inadequate; even more inadequate than he had been made to feel yesterday when he dropped the milk jug, left his scarf on the bus and trod on next door's kitten's tail. Sighing, Tim retired to his room and got on with his secret hobby, which was inventing games.

At the present moment Tim was working on a game called REDUNDO. Two or more players shook dice and moved round a board with the object of being first to get a job. There were various aids and obstacles on the way, such as: 'New soap factory opens—move forward three squares' or 'More local government cuts—go back to DOLE'. The snag was, it was difficult to add refinements to the game without actually playing it properly, and so far Tim was the only player. He badly needed advice and encouragement. Tim had hoped to recruit his friend Doggo Barker, but Tim's mother would not let Doggo penetrate any further than the kitchen, so that was that. Tim had no intention of fetching his game into the kitchen. He had vowed that his family must never set eyes on the REDUNDO board until he had sold it to a top toy manufacturer for at least a four-figure sum. That would show them! That would prove who was adequate and who wasn't! Tim's dad might well have a hush-hush job at the Helmuth Research Establishment (as Tim's mother was fond of reminding the neighbours) but that did not mean to say Lewis Evans was a genius. He was probably just the test-tube washer-up for some top scientist, or the bloke who mixed the guard-dogs' dinners. No wonder he would never talk about his work.

'Tim!' Mrs Evans yelled up the stairs. 'Your Uncle Cyril's here! Come and say hello to your Uncle Cyril.'

Tim trudged reluctantly downstairs. This interruption had cost him another great idea. He had just been about to write: 'Miners' strike—miss seven throws'. Or should it be: 'Teachers' go-slow—move forward two'? He couldn't quite decide which. At this rate his parents weren't going to live to see his triumph.

'Now then, Tim!' boomed Uncle Cyril, slapping the poor lad heartily on the shoulder.

'Hi, Uncle Cyril!' mumbled Tim, wincing with pain.

'I'm not all *that* high; only six foot one!' Uncle Cyril guffawed. Tim should have known better than to give him the opportunity for one of his terrible jokes.

'Well now,' Uncle Cyril went on, ignoring the stony silence, 'I've just been reading an ad. in the paper for your school's Music Festival. I don't mind coming to hear you sing in the choir, so you can sell me a couple of tickets if you like.'

'I'm not *in* the choir,' said Tim.

'Not in the choir?' cried Uncle Cyril, aghast. 'And you with a name like Evans? Let me tell you, your dad sang in the *Messiah* every Christmas until you were born.' Turning to Tim's mother, he asked: 'Why isn't he in the choir?'

Mrs Evans scowled at Tim. 'Well, why aren't you in

the choir?'

'Because I can't sing,' said Tim.

'CAN'T SING? Three generations of Welsh blood on his dad's side, and he can't sing?' Uncle Cyril looked ready to collapse.

'Of course he can sing!' snapped Mrs Evans. 'He's just lazy, that's all. Can't be bothered to go to the rehearsals. He'd rather shut himself up in his bedroom with a bundle of daft comics.'

'I'm going out,' said Tim. 'I'm going round to Doggo's.'

'And I don't know why you can't call that boy by his proper name. Eustace, isn't it? Your tea will be ready in half an hour, so don't you dare be late.'

Tim slammed the door as hard as he could, and was rewarded with a shaft of dazzling inspiration. 'World War Three breaks out—move forward twenty spaces.' Or better still: 'World War Three breaks out—drop dead!'

2

The Wrong Shop

On his way to Doggo's, Tim had to pass the 'FAIR GAME' shop window. The centre-piece of the window display was a set of tall ivory chessmen coloured red and white. Behind that was suspended a larger-than-life Monopoly board with a brimming bucket of Monopoly money underneath it, and crossed billiard-cues at either side. Around the rest of the window lay various other games in brightly-coloured boxes; packs of cards; table tennis outfits; shuttlecocks; yoyos; roulette wheels and giant dice.

Tim could not help stopping to stare, and soon all sorts of exciting possibilities were bouncing about his brain, sparking off a bright hallucination. The chessmen were gone, and there instead lay his REDUNDO board with intricate carvings of the characterful unemployed plodding their way to salvation across brilliantly-coloured squares.

Tim sighed deeply through a wistful smile. Then the chessmen swam back into focus—and on an impulse, Tim hurried into the shop.

Sam Snyder, the proprietor, was gift-wrapping a

179

Ludo game for a kind old lady who must be someone's great-granny. He frowned at Tim over the string-dispenser, forcefully conveying the impression that he knew exactly what Tim would be up to, given half a chance, but he needn't think he would get away with it. Tim fidgeted among the books—(*Pukka Poker; Mah-Jongg for the Million; Pontoon, Bridge and Other Diversions*)—whilst great-granny scrabbled in her handbag for cheque-book and pen. By the time she had altered the date on the cheque, turned out all her pockets for the bank-card and verified the price another twice, Tim had lost his courage and was slinking towards the door. But that made Sam Snyder suspicious. By now, the lad probably had a ping-pong ball up each sleeve and a pocketful of best quality Fetherflite darts.

'Hey, you! Come here!'

Tim swung round to face the counter, blushing as guiltily as if he had planned to mug great-granny on her way out.

'What do you want then, eh?' Sam Snyder was busy frisking Tim with his eyes whilst the old lady tottered happily on her way.

Tim took a deep breath, which steadied his nerve and gave him time to think. At last he managed to blurt out:

'I've invented a game!'

'Oh you have, have you?' Sam Snyder's sarcasm

could have felled a sturdy oak. 'Well, go and play it, then.'

The doorbell was already pinging with the next bona fide customer, which Tim patently was not.

But now, having gathered his courage, Tim did not intend to leave without some sort of satisfaction. He drew from his pocket a dog-eared, grubby sheet of much-folded paper, which he laid reverently on the counter.

'It's called REDUNDO. These are the rules and stuff. I know you're busy, Mr Snyder, but I'll call back later today when you've had time to read it, and I'll bring the board. I'll have managed to finish it by then.'

So saying, Tim fled, colliding with the incoming customer who lurched into a Magnetic Fishing set, sending shoals of little metal fish in a frantic surge to freedom.

Sam Snyder's eyes turned upwards to the giant frisbee hanging from the ceiling. 'Kids!' he exclaimed, screwing up the precious sheet of REDUNDO rules and hurling it into his waste-bin.

3

First Tastes of Human Error

''Uman error, that's what ruins everything,' declared Mrs Figgins from next door. 'You've only to look at aeroplanes. They can fill 'em up with all this clever stuff like radars and black boxes and I-don't-know-what, but if the pilot drops his glasses, or chokes on a fish-bone, you've had it! What I say is, you can't get away from 'uman error wherever you go.'

Tim's mother shivered. She had been telling Mrs Figgins that they were thinking of going to Spain for a holiday next summer, but now she was not so sure. The Evans family were new to the mysteries of flying, and maybe things had better stay that way.

'Yes, well—I'm just going round to the supermarket,' decided Mrs Evans in an attempt to get rid of her caller.

Mrs Figgins snorted loudly. 'Huh! Now there's 'uman error if ever I saw it! All them fancy machines for adding up your bill and taking away your change, and what happens? Daft girl hits the wrong keys and you get diddled. 'Uman error, that's what!' Her eyes narrowed as she added darkly, 'Let's hope there's none of it up at Hellmouth, that's all I can say!'

'Hellmouth' was the local nickname for the Helmuth Research Establishment where Tim's dad worked, and where it was suspected, but by no means confirmed, that lethal germs were being manufactured which could wipe out the whole of Russia some windy weekend.

Suddenly Mrs Figgins spotted Tim, who was hunched in an armchair reading his *Dandy*.

'Why can't he go to the supermarket for you?'

'Oh, you know what boys are. He's too lazy, that's why.'

'You never asked me!' protested Tim indignantly. 'I'll go if you like.'

'No thanks! We don't want to be sending search parties out. We want our dinner today, not next week. Anyway, if we're talking about human error. . . . '

Tim did not wait to hear any more. He threw his comic down disgustedly and marched off to collect his anorak. He would nip round to the 'FAIR GAME' shop and see if Mr Snyder had had time to look at REDUNDO yet. After all, he had had the board for a whole day now.

Mr Snyder was alone in the shop, re-packing a set of top quality, genuine wooden draughts which a customer had examined and rejected. He was cross to start with, and his mood did not improve when Tim asked

eagerly, 'Did you have time to look at it, then?'

'Look at what?'

'My game—REDUNDO.'

'Oh, that! What do *you* think, son?'

'You mean, you haven't even . . . ?'

'Look, laddie, I'm supposed to be running a business here, not a Citizens' Advice Bureau. That doorbell never stops pinging from morning to night.'

'It's not pinging now,' Tim pointed out reasonably enough.

Mr Snyder flushed a dull red. 'Cheeky young scamp! Go on, clear out of it!'

'I want my game back first.'

'Well, it'll be where you left it.'

Tim looked down the side of the counter, where he remembered having propped his board, but it was not there.

'It's gone!'

'Well, somebody's pinched it, then. I certainly haven't moved it.'

Tim's bitter disappointment was succeeded by alarm. 'They can't have pinched it! You don't understand—it's very important, is that board. I've got to have it back.'

'Shouldn't have left it there, then, should you? *I* didn't ask you to. I can't be responsible for stuff left lying in the shop. I lose enough of my own stock to shoplifters, and that's a fact.'

'Shoplifters?' Tim's voice had taken on a note of horror. 'You mean, a shoplifter's taken my board? Well, have you any idea who it could have been, Mr Snyder? Which customers were in the shop yesterday?'

'Now, that's a daft question, isn't it, son? Be reasonable! Do you think Father Christmas can remember what he's put down every chimney? 'Course he can't! He's got too much on his mind, like me.'

Tim clutched at this thread of hope. 'In that case—

suppose you had so much on your mind that you moved my board without thinking? You could have tidied it away with some other boards. Sort of—a case of human error.'

Sam Snyder found that idea downright insulting. 'I'll give you a taste of human error, you young monkey!' He started forward with goodness knows what fell purpose in mind, but just then a delivery man staggered in with two dozen sets of 'Scrabble' and a box of spinning-tops, and Tim was lost sight of in the rush.

4

Dark Suspicions

Doggo Barker was on the playing field, swinging from a piece of his mother's clothes-line which he had attached to a tree.

'Hey, Doggo!' Tim had to shout three times to attract his friend's attention. 'Want to come and help me catch a shoplifter?' It was a desperately anxious invitation.

'Too easy!' boasted Doggo. 'There's more shoplifters in the world than proper customers.' All the same, Doggo jumped down from his rope, which managed to

189

swing wide and slap backwards on to Tim, catching him right across the neck.

'Ooops! Sorry!'

'Hey, that hurt!' A great red weal immediately began to rise on Tim's neck, which he fingered tenderly as he told the tale of the missing REDUNDO board.

Doggo was not impressed. 'Can't you make another? Surely you've not forgotten already what you put on it? We've plenty of cardboard at our house, and you can borrow our Eileen's felt-tips.'

'It wasn't cardboard; it was a good piece of formica I found under some rubbish at the back of our shed, and I stuck proper drawing paper over it. Anyway, that's not the point. If I don't get that board back, somebody else could pinch my idea. It's worth a fortune.'

'Gerraway!' grinned Doggo.

'It's true! You know the bloke who invented "Monopoly"? He's a multi-millionaire now.'

'Sure he is!' Doggo's grin widened.

'Honestly, he's shovelling money in. And my game's as good as that, if not better. Anybody who know anything about games will tell you.'

'Sam Snyder doesn't seem to have been very taken with it.'

'He never even looked at it.'

Doggo's eyes suddenly brightened. 'How do you know he didn't?'

'He said so, didn't he?'

'Yeah, and he once told me he'd sold out of fireworks when I knew bloomin' well he hadn't. Just because our Eileen put a banger through his letter-box.'

'You mean . . . ?'

'I mean, suppose Sam Snyder's the one who's pinched your game? He'd know just what to do with it, an' all. He'd know how to set about getting a patent, or whatever you call it, so that nobody can copy it. He'd know how to have all the boards and pieces properly

made and dished out round all the games shops. He'd even know how to advertise it. For a bloke in his position, all that sort of stuff would be as easy as falling off one of his own warpy old skateboards. You could be buying a REDUNDO set yourself in a few weeks' time, and Snyder would be raking in the profits.'

'Never!' yelled Tim, adding, with less conviction, 'Do you reckon?'

'Believe me, it's the only answer. Nobody else but Snyder would think of such a thing, and anyway, nobody else could ever have sneaked out of that shop with a great board under their arm and not be spotted by beady-eyed Sam.'

Tim looked stunned. There was a long, agonising pause before he said:

'Well, that's fraud and stealing and a lot besides, and he needn't think he's going to get away with it. I'll show him!'

'That's the spirit!' grinned Doggo, relishing the prospect of battle. 'Now you're talking!'

'I'll murder him!' growled Tim, already rushing off in the direction of 'FAIR GAME'. But Doggo dragged him to a halt. 'Hang about! You can't just go barging in there, chucking accusations around. He'll only deny them. You want a proper plan. In fact, what you want to do is frighten him into a confession. It's the only way.'

Wild as he was, Tim could not help feeling this idea was even wilder. Nothing would frighten Sam Snyder, except possibly the Income Tax man. But Doggo went on thoughtfully, 'You could do it, an' all! If I had a "highly secret" dad like you have, I'd frighten Snyder all right.'

'What do you mean, a "highly secret" dad? He's not a bloomin' spy.'

'He works at Hellmouth, doesn't he? Who know what goes on behind them armed patrols and electrified fences and remote-controlled gates? If you played your cards right, you could reduce old Snyder to a trembling blob of jelly.'

'Oh, yeah!' sneered Tim. 'I could borrow my dad's Death Ray out of the bathroom cabinet.'

'Hey—that remark's not as daft as you think! It's just given me an idea.'

Tim groaned, and was about to protest that he would have nothing to do with Doggo's idea, when suddenly Mrs Evans and Aunt Maisie hove into view.

'Told you where he'd be, didn't I?' Aunt Maisie cried.

'Here, our Tim!' shouted Mrs Evans angrily. 'Have you gone off with that piece of formica that your dad was going to fix on top of my washer? Because if you have, you can jolly well fetch it back, double-quick.'

Before Tim could reply, Aunt Maisie shrieked:

'Oooh, what's he done to his neck?'

'What *have* you done to your neck?' Tim's mother asked Tim.

'I tried to hang myself,' mumbled Tim, 'but it didn't work, worse luck!'

5

Instant Death

'Whatever's this, then?' Tim asked, as Doggo emerged
from his house clutching a bottle of dark green liquid.

'Shampoo.'

'Well, we're not going to scare anybody with that.'

'Don't you be too sure!' Doggo turned the bottle
round so that Tim could read the label. At the top was
a garish picture of a multi-coloured skull-and-cross-
bones over the bright red letters: 'GLOLOX'. Under
that, in two lines of thick black type, were the words:

INSTANT DEATH
TO DANDRUFF!

Doggo's dad ran the local barber's shop and often
brought home free samples of shampoos and various
other hair preparations that travellers had tried to
persuade him to use. This one was the very latest, not
yet on the market.

'If we cut the bottom line off that label,' Doggo
explained, 'Sam Snyder won't know this stuff from
Nitro-Glycerine or Plague-Infested Gooseberry Wine.

We'll just drop the merest hint that you may have pinched it from your dad, who works at Hell-mouth . . . .'

'But my dad wouldn't bring anything home from there. They get searched all the time. They even check on his sandwich box.'

'So what? Sam Snyder's not to know that, is he? He'll think your dad sneaked the INSTANT DEATH out to sell to the IRA or something. It's my bet Snyder will give us the benefit of the doubt *and* your REDUNDO board when he sees that bottle.'

'You're mad!' exploded Tim. 'You can't go around threatening folks like that.'

'Who's threatening folks? It's only shampoo.'

'Well, you'd never get away with it. And anyway, you'd land my dad in a right load of trouble.'

'It's nothing to do with your dad. My dad's more likely to be in trouble than yours if anything goes wrong. But nothing's going to go wrong.'

'That's all *you* know! Suppose you do happen to scare Snyder, and he hands my board back? What's he going to do then? As soon as we've left the shop he's going to ring up the police and tell them there's a deadly bottle at large from Hellmouth and my dad's pinched it.'

'He won't do that. Because as soon as we've got your board back we'll explain it was just a joke. Sam Snyder runs a games shop. He's in the entertainments business, isn't he? So he should be able to see the funny side.'

'*You* should be in the entertainment business,' grumbled Tim. 'You could earn a living making up tall stories for fifth-rate comics.'

'You're not *scared* of Snyder, by any chance, are you?' grinned Doggo.

'Me? Scared?'

They argued on for a while, Tim suggesting (and Doggo demolishing) more and more possible snags, until in the end Tim began to think his REDUNDO game just wasn't worth the fuss. It was a failure, like everything else he had ever tried to do. How could he have thought that anybody, least of all Sam Snyder, would want to steal it? Bitterly disillusioned and in a thoroughly bad temper, Tim finally turned his back on Doggo and the green bottle, and marched off home.

When he got there, he found Mrs Figgins explaining to his mother over the front fence that a neighbour had just been rushed to hospital after eating what she had thought were mushrooms.

'A terrible case of 'uman error,' Mrs Figgins was explaining with grim satisfaction. Then she spotted Tim, and cried in thunderstruck surprise: 'Well, bless us, here's your Tim! Why's he moping about with nothing to do, on a nice day like this?'

'Why are you moping about with nothing to do?' Tim's mother asked Tim. 'You could be finding that formica, for a start.'

Whereupon Tim's face changed from dull angry red to bright angry red, and he turned and marched back the way he had just come, calling rudely over his shoulder: 'As a matter of fact, I've got plenty to do. Me and Doggo's just started a Reign of Terror.'

'Cheek!' Mrs Evans called after him. 'You wait till your dad comes home!'

6

Even More Instant Death

Sam Snyder was sorting Bingo cards into bundles of twenty, but at the sound of the doorbell he looked up. Tim and Doggo edged cautiously into the shop, Doggo deftly turning the OPEN sign to CLOSED behind his back.

Sam Snyder frowned with instant suspicion, but before he had time to utter a word Doggo whipped out the bottle from underneath his anorak and placed it strategically on the counter.

'Oh, not you again!' Sam Snyder groaned at Tim.

'You remember him and his REDUNDO board, then?' began Doggo pleasantly, swivelling the INSTANT DEATH label round to a spot where Sam's gaze was bound to fall upon it.

'Remember his board? I've never had the chance to forget it!' spluttered Sam. 'But I can promise you this, if I hear any more about it there'll be trouble. I've already told you I don't know what's happened to it. So you can go away and stop pestering me. And take that sticky bottle of bubble-blower with you.'

'Bubble-blower?' shrieked Doggo in indignant disbelief. 'That's not bubble-blower. . . . '

But he got no further, for suddenly a curtain at the rear of the shop was swished aside and a plump, warm, beaming Mrs Snyder bounced into view.

'Couldn't help overhearing,' she admitted. 'And maybe I can help if you're looking for a board. I found one lying about when I was vacuuming the shop. It didn't look like genuine stock; it had no name or address on, and it was in the way. So I threw it out.'

'Threw it out?' echoed Tim, aghast.

'Well, I propped it up against the dustbin; it was too big to fit inside. You could have had it back, son, only they've been for the rubbish this morning. I'm ever so sorry!'

Tim's shoulders sagged. 'Oh well, that's that, then!' He was now prepared to forget the whole thing, having at least been reassured that his idea was not stolen. Some day, perhaps, he could start again.

'No need for you to apologise,' Sam told his wife sternly. 'It was the lad's own fault for leaving that board where he did. Kids are far too pushy and cheeky these days. Think they can do just what they like.' He seized the GLOLOX bottle and waved it in the air. 'There's an example! Look at that, plonked down without a thought! It's left a great, sticky patch on my counter, has that!' Still clutching the bottle, Sam dived under the counter for a cloth to wipe up the mess.

Meantime, Mrs Snyder had her eye on Tim. 'Oh, bless him! He's upset!' she crooned sympathetically. 'I never thought that board would mean so much to anybody or I wouldn't have thrown it out. Invented it yourself, did you, son? Well, if it's any comfort, you did all right, except that people don't want to make fun of tragedies like unemployment. You'll have to think of a fresh idea. But keep trying, because I reckon you've a flair!'

Tim looked up in amazement. Mrs Snyder had actually liked his game! He could not remember anybody ever praising him before and could not stop himself blushing with pleasure. She was wrong about REDUNDO being too tragic, though. What could be more tragic than hounding a king to death, as in chess; or being told to GO TO JAIL; or falling prey to some nasty, deadly snake, just when you're at the top of your ladder?

'Tell you what, why don't you two come through and have a glass of orange juice and a slice of cake? It's the least I can do to make up for what I can only describe as a genuine human error.'

Mrs Snyder held the curtain aside invitingly, affording a glimpse of a comfortable sitting-room with plenty of fat, shiny cushions, plastic roses in a vase and a radio softly playing. As the boys seemed hesitant, she encouraged them: 'Don't mind my husband! His bark's worse than his bite. I expect he's mad at himself for not keeping a better eye on your game.'

Sam, rising up from the depths of the counter like the Loch Ness Monster, protested loudly at this, belligerently brandishing the GLOLOX. That was the moment at which his wife first caught sight of the bottle. She froze in mid-sentence and turned pale, eyes widening in a horrified face. Then, with an awful moan, she half-collapsed against the wall, pointing with trembling finger at the dark green bottle.

'P-put it d-down carefully, S-Sam,' she managed to stammer. 'D-don't bang it or j-jerk it about.'

'Oh, it's all right,' Tim reassured his new friend. 'It's only shampoo.'

Doggo glared murderously at Tim, but Mrs Snyder was not listening. She was staring at her husband in pure terror and whispering: 'The news-flash! Didn't you hear the news-flash?'

'How could I hear a news-flash when I've been in the shop all morning?' Sam snapped irritably. 'What news-flash? What are you talking about?'

Mrs Snyder took a shaky breath. 'You know they've got couriers at Helmuth, running messages for the scientists? Well, one of them couriers disappeared this morning when he was out delivering a bottle full of highly dangerous dark green liquid. It didn't say what the stuff actually was, but they were making such a fuss,

it must be something terrible. They said nobody was to touch that bottle if they found it, not for love nor money!' She turned distractedly to the boys. 'Where did you pick it up?'

'I don't believe this!' Doggo groaned, glimpsing what could have been wonderful possibilities.

But Tim retorted, '*I* do! It's just my rotten sort of luck!'

7

Tragedy Strikes Home

There was only one thing to do, and Doggo did it. He grabbed the bottle (which Sam Snyder had set down in bewilderment on the counter) and fled, dragging Tim with him before the lad had time to protest. They were halfway to Doggo's house by the time Mr Snyder had finished dialling 999.

'What do we do now?' Tim wondered miserably. 'We aren't half going to be in trouble. It was stupid to run off with the bottle like that. It just makes us look

guilty.' His chief regret was that nice Mrs Snyder, who had taken an interest in him, must now regard him as a loathsome, despicable terrorist.

'We haven't done anything wrong that I know of,' maintained Doggo stubbornly. 'We never even made any threats. We didn't have a chance. All we did was plonk a bottle of shampoo down on Sam Snyder's counter. If he thought it was something else, that's his look-out. And how were we to know some daft courier was going to lose his bottle at the same time? Proper careless, he must have been.'

'Yeah, I hope he gets his share of what's coming,' Tim said bitterly. 'He deserves the sack and at least ten years in the Tower of London.'

'Good thing I kept that strip of label when I cut it off,' said Doggo. 'Did a very neat job on that with one of my dad's special shop razor-blades. All we have to do now is to stick the strip on again, put the shampoo back in our bathroom cabinet and lie low.'

'Lie low where?'

Doggo thought for a minute, then he said: 'There's one place that's pretty deserted in the holidays, and that's school. We could hide in there for a bit, just till they've found their precious bottle. The fuss will soon die down then, and they might even forget about us altogether.'

'School will be locked up,' said Tim, who was by no

means eager to go back there before he had to. But Doggo thought they could manage to get in somehow.

'Leave it to me!' he said.

However, by now Tim was thoroughly fed up. Enough had been left to Doggo as it was, and look where his efforts had got them!

'Why don't we just go and confess, and get it over with?' Tim suggested gloomily.

'Who to? The police? You must be joking!' Doggo could scarcely believe his ears. 'I'm not confessing to anything, especially when I haven't done it.'

'Well, all right, let's do something positive instead of just crawling into a hole and hiding. Something that will put us in the right again with everyone. Let's find that missing courier—and the bottle. They must be around here somewhere.'

'Hey!' cried Doggo, brightening. 'That's not a bad idea! Might be quite an adventure, in fact.' He looked at his watch. 'There's a news bulletin in ten minutes. Maybe that will tell us more about it, so that we'll know where to start looking.' He ran into the house and turned on the radio.

The two of them fretted impatiently through a whole dreary weather forecast, and an even drearier political wrangle, before the item was even mentioned, but at last there it was.

'Late this morning it was reported that a courier

208

from the highly secret Helmuth Research Establishment had failed to keep an assignment at the companion laboratory on the moors between Whitsend and Doomsbury. It is believed that his car, which was delivering a bottle of highly dangerous liquid, was hijacked, the courier taken hostage and the bottle stolen. The car was later found abandoned in a remote spot on the moors.' There then followed a description of the bottle and a warning not to handle it if it was found. 'Anyone with any information about the earlier movements of this white Mini Metro registration number. . . .'

Doggo, ready with pen and paper, began eagerly scribbling down the registration number, but before he had finished Tim was careering round the room like a lunatic.

'That's my dad's car!' he was shouting. 'My dad must be that courier! He's been kidnapped!'

'Oh, no! It's one bloomin' shock after another!' moaned Doggo. 'What was it you wished on that courier? The sack and at least ten years in the Tower of London?'

'Stop clowning—my dad could be dead!' yelled Tim, who was desperately trying to take in all this staggering information. He had not even known his dad was a courier, and now there Mr Evans was, in the power of some madman with a genuine bottle of

Instant Death, while Tim's mother stood poised on the verge of widowhood. The most sickening thing about it was that Tim could not help feeling it was all his fault.

8
Reign of Terror

Tim ran home at once, followed at a respectful distance by Doggo, who did not want to intrude upon the family's grief but felt he would like to be near, just in case he could help. So Doggo hung around the Evans' garden gate chewing his nails and kicking bits of gravel, while Tim rushed into the house.

Aunt Maisie and Uncle Cyril were in the kitchen, commiserating with Tim's mother.

'Came round right away to see what we could do,' said Uncle Cyril, all solemn for once.

'Well, you can keep Mrs Figgins out for a start,' Tim's mother wailed hysterically as she spotted an eager face hovering outside the kitchen window.

'Would you like me to drive up on to the moors and look for Lewis?'

'That's a super idea, Uncle Cyril! Me and Doggo will come with you.'

Since Mrs Evans was too upset by now to offer an opinion—and in fact was being led off to bed by Aunt Maisie—away went Cyril and Tim, collecting Doggo at the gate.

'I don't know about taking you kids,' Uncle Cyril worried. 'We might run into trouble.'

'Three pairs of eyes are better than one,' said Tim. 'And your own eyes will be watching the road, anyway. Doggo and me can look out of both sides of the car, and if Dad's up there we'll spot him.'

'I've got really good eyesight,' Doggo claimed. 'My mum once said she reckoned I'd got double vision.'

'That was when you said you'd given her twenty pence change instead of tenpence,' Tim reminded him, but he said it quietly so that Uncle Cyril could not hear.

'All right—get in, then!' Uncle Cyril had just opened the rear door of his car when a police vehicle drew up on the opposite side of the road.

Another half-minute, and they could have been away!

'Excuse me, sir,' a police officer addressed himself politely to Uncle Cyril, 'but we're looking for two boys named Timothy Evans and'—here he consulted his notebook incredulously—'Eustace Barker. As you have just emerged from Timothy Evans's house accompanied by two young gentlement in the correct age-range, I assume . . . .'

'You assume right, officer,' sighed Uncle Cyril. Turning to the boys, he asked what the dickens they had been up to now.

The police officer explained. 'I'm afraid I shall have

to ask them to accompany me to the station. Just routine, you understand, sir; probably all a waste of time, but in a case of national security we have to make absolutely sure.'

'Honest, officer, it was only shampoo!' insisted Doggo for the umpteenth time. 'I can run home and fetch the bottle if you like.'

'We *have* got lots of shampoo at our house,' agreed Doggo's mother, who had had to be fetched before the police questioning could begin. 'Though I must say I never noticed any missing.'

'That's because I put it back,' said Doggo.

'What did you want shampoo for, anyway?' his mother could not help asking. In normal circumstances she practically had to tie Doggo to the sink before he would consent to having his hair washed.

'We were going to blow bubbles with it.'

The police officer grinned, which made Doggo feel even more shame-faced. Blowing bubbles was kids' stuff. But what else could Doggo have said? He only hoped that Tim, being interrogated in another room, would be inspired to give the same answer.

Alas! Tim had crumpled under the weight of grief and guilt. He had lost his dad, his game and his only adult ally, Mrs Snyder; and he wished he had never heard of GLOLOX. To crown it all, on the way here in the police car, when he was helpless to do anything about it, he had spotted four dustmen rattling a dice-shaker excitedly round his REDUNDO board as they took their tea-break on a grass verge. In a scarcely audible voice, Tim admitted miserably:

'That bottle was a sort of blackmail.'

'Blackmail, eh?'

The police officer, who had just read a rambling

report from the policewoman sent to see Tim's pros-
trate mother, now frowned thoughtfully at the long,
red weal on Tim's neck.

'I suppose this is all part of the Reign of Terror your
mother's been going on about?'

9

Eureka!

In the police station there was a sudden flurry of activity. An important telephone message had just come in. Lewis Evans, the missing Helmuth courier, had turned up at his destination after all, several hours late but still in possession of the all-important bottle. What is more, he was claiming not to have been hi-jacked at all. Such a tale, he insisted, was too fantastic for words. Yet the tale he eventually told to reporters who swarmed into the laboratory was even more fantastic.

Lewis Evans possessed, he explained modestly, a fine tenor voice and had often sung in such great works as Handel's *Messiah*. But lately, what with shift-work and family commitments and jobs around the house (like fitting a formica top on his wife's washer, for instance) he didn't have time to belong to a choir. So whenever his day's assignment took him up on to the moors—as it often did, Helmuth's companion laboratory being situated between Whitsend and Doomsbury—he would get out of the car for ten minutes or so at the remotest spot he could find, fill his lungs with good, clean air and then let rip with a couple of arias, or the 'Soldiers' Chorus' from *Faust*, a practice which disturbed nobody but the sheep.

That was exactly what he had done today. The only difference was that today he had accidentally locked his keys in the car when he got out to sing, and had therefore had to walk the last, long, difficult moorland stretch to the laboratory, sinking up to his knees in a peat-bog on the way. Luckily, the Helmuth product,

the vital bottle, had been nestling safely in his jacket pocket all the time, and had been duly delivered.

'Wasn't that a dangerous thing to do?' an outraged reporter cried. 'Gallivanting about on craggy, boggy moors with a lethal bottle in your pocket?'

'Downright irresponsible, I call it!' another reporter shouted, to a chorus of 'hear, hear's.

Whereupon Lewis, looking genuinely puzzled, cried, 'Lethal? What's so lethal about a cure for the common cold? Even if it does turn out to be another dud?'

Well!

There had been, it seemed a mix-up. Some over-worked publicity officer at Helmuth had given out the wrong information in a panic when Lewis Evans was first reported missing. It turned out to be another member of staff, a Leonard Evans, now happily on his way to Porton Down, who was actually in charge of the dark green lethal stuff.

Of course he was! The really dangerous stuff, as Lewis Evans later assured the world in a television interview, was not shuttled around the country in Mini Metros, but packed inside well-lined, well-protected crates in special spill-proof vans.

'They wouldn't trust me with it, in any case,' he was forced to admit. 'I'm only a Courier Grade Four, not Grade One like Leonard Evans.'

219

Tim, who was sampling the novelty of watching his own dad on television, felt a sudden leap of the spirits at this. That would put paid to his mother's smug hints to the neighbours! 'Courier Grade Four' was a far cry from the Chief Research Scientist she was always trying to suggest. In fact, 'Courier Grade Four' was barely adequate for making one's mark on the world at all, television interviews notwithstanding. Surely Tim could do better than that? A tiny bubble of euphoria rose somewhere in the depths of Tim and began to work its way upwards towards his brain.

'So, are we to understand, then,' the television interviewer was now demanding of Lewis Evans, 'that this whole unfortunate episode, this full-scale panic, this numbing shock to an already nervous nation, was nothing more than a couple of stupid mistakes?'

Tim's dad grinned sheepishly at the camera.

'Afraid so!' he admitted. 'You'll just have to look on it as a double dose of simple human error. After all, that's life in a nutshell, isn't it?'

This was the moment at which the bubble reached Tim's brain and burst like the Dawn of Enlightenment. Radiant, he leapt from his seat, projecting his arms, his whole body, his very soul in a joyous 'Hallelujah Chorus' towards the ceiling.

For Tim Evans had just thought of a wonderful new game called UMANERRA. Two or more players

shook dice and moved around a board, attempting to reach OLD AGE without lighting upon any one of a number of 'human error' obstacles, ranging in stupidity and horror from . . . .

Tim reached eagerly for pen and paper.